"Reid...what's wrong?" Claire asked.

"I don't know." He started turning his horse in a slow circle. "Did you hear that?"

"Hear what?"

"It sounds like...bees."

Claire could hear it now, along with see a tinge of smoke in the air. A streak of orange shot out in front of Reid, jerking her attention back to the left.

"Head to the tree line, Claire. *Now.* It's some kind of drone."

Flame-throwing drones could be used to clear power lines and do agriculture burns. But this...this was clearly an attack.

Claire heard the crackle of flames as the drone shot out another fire trail. Orange heat crackled behind her. A row of bushes caught fire.

"Whoa, boy...you're okay." She worked to calm her own agitated horse while trying to keep her balance on the saddle.

The buzzing of the drone swooped down again as Reid raced toward her. Another ball of flames shot out from the spiderlike contraption. A second later, Reid lost his grip and was thrown off his horse...

Lisa Harris is a Christy Award winner and winner of the Best Inspirational Suspense Novel for 2011 from *RT Book Reviews*. She and her family are missionaries in southern Africa. When she's not working, she loves hanging out with her family, cooking different ethnic dishes, photography and heading into the African bush on safari. For more information about her books and life in Africa, visit her website at lisaharriswrites.com.

Books by Lisa Harris

Love Inspired Suspense

Final Deposit
Stolen Identity
Deadly Safari
Taken
Desperate Escape
Desert Secrets
Fatal Cover-Up
Deadly Exchange
No Place to Hide
Sheltered by the Soldier
Christmas Witness Pursuit
Hostage Rescue
Christmas Up in Flames

Visit the Author Profile page at Harlequin.com.

CHRISTMAS UP IN FLAMES

LISA HARRIS

LOVE INSPIRED SUSPENSE
INSPIRATIONAL ROMANCE

LOVE INSPIRED® SUSPENSE
INSPIRATIONAL ROMANCE

ISBN-13: 978-1-335-40324-7

Recycling programs for this product may not exist in your area.

Christmas Up in Flames

This edition published by arrangement with Harlequin Books S.A.

For questions and comments about the quality of this book, please contact us at CustomerService@Harlequin.com.

Love Inspired
22 Adelaide St. West, 40th Floor
Toronto, Ontario M5H 4E3, Canada
www.Harlequin.com

Printed in U.S.A.

Trust in the Lord with all thine heart;
and lean not unto thine own understanding.
In all thy ways acknowledge Him,
and He shall direct thy paths.
–Proverbs 3:5-6

To my in-laws, who have always been there for me,
and who have taught me so much about love
and the importance of family.

ONE

The piercing sound of the fire alarm jerked Claire Holiday from her dreams. She stumbled out of bed automatically, almost tripping over a desk chair in the dark. She had to get to Owen. She fought to clear her mind. No. Her son wasn't here. He was safe with her mother.

She hurried across the unfamiliar room of the bed-and-breakfast and headed for the door. A hint of smoke tinged the air, but chances were that someone had gone down to the kitchen for a snack, burned something and set off the alarm. Still, she of all people knew how fast a fire could spread. In thirty seconds, a small flame could quickly become a major blaze. In just a few short minutes, a house could be filled with smoke and engulfed in flames. And instead of lighting the way, fires produced thick black smoke that could not only leave you blinded to where to go, but could kill you with toxic gases.

She took in a breath and choked. The second-floor room was starting to fill with smoke. Any lingering brain fog from being asleep vanished in an instant. This was no small kitchen fire. She needed to get out.

She touched the doorknob to make sure it wasn't hot, then turned the handle.

It moved, but the door wouldn't budge.

How was that possible?

She tugged on the handle again, but the door still wouldn't open. Her mind worked to solve the problem as she pounded on the door, shelving any panic that threatened to erupt. Someone would hear her. There were three other rooms on this floor of the B&B, and at least one of them was occupied.

"Help! Someone…please."

She drew in another breath and her lungs filled with more smoke. With her eyes now adjusted to the darkness, she ran back to the bed and dragged one of the blankets onto the floor, then shoved it against the bottom of the door in order to slow down the smoke seeping into the room.

Her mind worked quickly for a solution. If she couldn't get out through the door, she'd climb through the window and onto the roof. Her fingers worked to unlock the window overlooking the south lawns of the large house, but she couldn't open it. She'd checked it out of habit when she first arrived. Hadn't she?

She needed her phone. She'd plugged it in to charge, which meant she'd left it on the bedside table. A second later, she scooped it up and called 911 as smoke continued to slowly creep in. She grabbed a washcloth that had been left for her, dipped it into the cup of water next to the bed and pressed the wet material to her face. That would at least slow down the effects of the smoke.

"Nine-one-one, what is the location of your emergency?" a woman asked her.

"This is Claire Holiday," she said, pulling the washcloth from her mouth. "I'm staying at the Timber Falls Bed and Breakfast. The house is on fire, and I'm trapped in my room."

"You're trapped in your room, ma'am?"

"Yes."

"We have the fire department on the way right now, but you need to try to get out of the room. Have you tried the door?"

"I've tried the door and the window. I don't know why, but they're both locked or jammed."

"I know this is frightening, but I need you to stay calm. Stay on the line and tell me exactly where you are in the house."

"I'm on the second floor." She felt her voice crack. She could see Owen grinning up at her, telling her to hold on, to keep fighting. She had to find a way out for his sake. She grabbed an iron candlestick off a shelf and started banging on the lock on the window, but it still wouldn't open. Smashing the glass wasn't safe. It would leave shards, and with the bars in place on the outside of the frame, it wasn't an escape option anyway. She needed to open it.

"Ma'am…are you still there?"

The smoke was getting worse in the room and her lungs were starting to burn.

"Yes… I'm here."

"What room are you in?"

"The second door on the…the north side of the house. Upstairs." She stared out the window and felt her heart pound inside her chest. "I can see flames engulfing the main structure of the house, and the fire is spreading quickly. How long until the fire department arrives?"

"I was just told they are ninety seconds out."

She frowned. It was taking too long, and she knew there were at least four other people in the house.

"There are other people staying here. Advise the local hospital to be ready and have paramedics here."

"Ma'am...we'll worry about coordinating help. My concern is to get you out of there safely. I'd like you to go try the door again."

Claire squeezed her eyes shut. "I told you it's locked somehow. It won't open."

"I understand, but I'd like you to try again. It's easy to panic in a situation like this—"

"I'm not panicking. It's jammed."

The woman was placating her, and yet Claire knew she was right. There was no reason for the door to be locked.

She obeyed the order and tried it again, but it still wouldn't budge.

"You said the window's jammed, as well?"

"Jammed...stuck...yes."

She wasn't sure anymore, which had to sound ridiculous. It sounded ridiculous to her too, made her want to question her state of mind. Why wouldn't it open? She squeezed her eyes shut and pressed the wet cloth against her face. A wave of dizziness swept through her. Was it from the smoke, or was something else at play here? She'd considered taking a couple of over-the-counter sleeping pills last night, just to ensure she got a good night's sleep. She'd been extra tired lately due to long hours, but no...she hadn't taken them, deciding that, for one, she was so tired she probably wouldn't have any trouble sleeping, and two, she didn't want to risk being foggy headed in the morning.

There was one other option. Could this somehow be connected to the string of arson fires she'd been investigating? Was that even possible?

She'd come to Timber Falls hunting an arsonist who'd been terrorizing the state for the past eighteen months, starting nine fires, killing two people and causing over four million dollars in damages. Authorities believed that there was a connection to a recent fire here in Timber Falls, and it was her job to find the arsonist before someone else got hurt. But was this fire connected or just a coincidence?

No. She walked back to the window. She didn't believe in coincidences. And she refused to be the third victim.

She could hear the sirens in the distance, wailing as they came down the narrow gravel road toward the house.

"I can hear the firetruck."

"Good. They should be there in less than a minute."

Claire's lungs burned as she flipped on her phone's flashlight and shone it around the room, worried there wasn't going to be enough time to get her out of this locked box.

"Claire… I want you to get down on the ground and lay still until we can get someone to the room. It will help protect you from the smoke you're breathing. Can you do that?"

"I am, but please…please hurry and get someone up here quickly."

She dropped down to the ground, still struggling to believe this was really happening. She always made an exit plan in every hotel she stayed in, every building she walked into. She taught people how to make a home fire escape plan so something like this didn't happen. She educated people to install smoke alarms, to ensure all doors and windows opened easily for a quick escape and to set meeting places for families in the event of a house fire.

The gases oozing through the cracks around the door were more dangerous than the fire. At first they disoriented you, then they made you sleepy. Carbon monoxide and hydrogen cyanide were silent killers. CO bonded with red blood cells, blocking them from carrying oxygen through the body, which was like suffocating from the inside out. Symptoms began within seconds. In the right circumstances, a person could be dead in a matter of minutes.

And now it was happening to her.

Owen... I'm so, so sorry, baby...

Her fingers pressed the cloth against her mouth as she lay on the floor. Was this what it was like to die in a fire? The initial fear morphing into panic when you realized there was no escape. Heat from the fire pressing in around you. Fighting for air. Fighting for every breath. She was starting to feel disoriented. Before long, she wouldn't be able to get up or keep her eyes open. How much time had passed? Four...maybe five minutes. It seemed like an eternity.

All she knew was that she didn't have much time left. One...maybe two minutes until the smoke completely engulfed her.

"Claire..." The 911 operator's voice pulled her back in. "Claire, can you hear me?"

"Yeah... I can hear you."

"You're going to be okay. Help is almost there."

She closed her eyes. Fifteen minutes of smoke with no oxygen would kill you. Five or ten minutes could cause brain damage. Her mother had never liked her career choice. People, no doubt, would find it interesting that the woman who died had been the investigator who'd come to Timber Falls to examine the latest fire presumed to be connected to the Rocky Mountain Arsonist, as they were calling him. But this wasn't how she was supposed to die. She was supposed to be the one who stopped things like this from happening.

She could hear the sound of wood splintering as the door broke away from the frame. Someone was here, rushing into the room. She tried to move, but felt frozen. She needed to call her mom, let her know she was sorry.

Someone shouted. If only she didn't feel so tired.

"Ma'am…"

Someone was in the room, talking to her.

"You're going to be okay. Just hang in there. I've got you now, and I'm going to get you out of here."

Reid O'Callaghan carried the woman out into the chilly December air, then laid her gently on a gurney in the semi-darkness. "She was trapped in a room on the second floor and is suffering from smoke inhalation."

"I'm fine." The woman fought to sit up. "I need to go check on—"

"No." Reid put his hands on her shoulders. "You need to lie still and let them treat you."

She fought against him, still trying to sit up. "There were other people in the house."

"Everyone is out safe and accounted for. You were the last one." Reid hesitated as familiar eyes stared back at him. "Wait a minute… Claire?"

A deluge of memories surfaced. Claire Holiday had been his first love, and the one woman he'd never been able to forget. What was she doing back in Timber Falls?

She looked up at him, clearly just as surprised to see him. "Reid… I—"

"What are you doing here?"

"I came for a job," she said, her voice raspy from the smoke.

"It's a pretty small town. If you were hoping to avoid me, this probably wasn't the way."

"You're a fireman."

"You forgot?"

"Of course not."

It was how they first met—training together in Denver.

"And you saved my life," she said.

But Claire Holiday wasn't a place he wanted to go. He'd broken off their relationship years ago. She'd been ready to settle down with him, but instead of asking her to marry him like he should have, he'd got cold feet and ran. When he eventually realized he'd made the wrong decision, it had been too late. She'd refused to take his calls or answer his texts, but it hadn't mattered in the end.

He'd never seen her again.

Until now.

"Reid, I—"

The paramedic laid her hand on Claire's arm. "I'm sorry, but you shouldn't be talking right now, and I need to get you hooked up to some oxygen. We'll get you to a hospital and checked out by a doctor, and *then* the two of you can catch up."

Claire nodded, finally lying back on the gurney without a fight.

"We're ready to go."

"Reid—"

He laid his hand on her shoulder. "You're not supposed to talk."

"Just one more thing. Thank you. For risking your life for me. The door was jammed and maybe the window, as well."

"Jammed…" He held up his hand to the paramedic, signaling for her to give them a moment. "What do you mean?"

"I couldn't get out."

"How is that possible?"

"I don't know."

"It would be normal to panic and miss something—"

"I didn't miss something. I was scared, but I never panicked."

His mind shifted back to the moment he'd tried to open the door to the room. He'd been told by the 911 operator that there was a woman trapped, but he'd assumed whoever was in there had simply panicked. He knew Claire, and she was right. She wouldn't have let the fire unnerve her. And the door…he'd had trouble opening it, which was why he'd ended up breaking it down.

Had it somehow really been jammed?

"Let them take care of you," he said. "I'll stop by the hospital and make sure you're okay. We can talk more about this then."

He stepped back from the ambulance, instantly regretting his words. What had he been thinking, telling her that he was going to visit her? He had nothing to say to her.

Captain Ryder walked up to him and squeezed his shoulder as the ambulance drove away. "Well done in there, Reid."

"Thanks."

"You saved that woman's life."

"All in a day's work."

The captain took a step backward. "Are you okay, man? You look a little pale."

"I'm fine. I just… I know her."

Knew her. Once, a long time ago.

"Claire Holiday?"

Reid nodded. "Yeah."

"She's here to investigate the fire out at the Reynolds farm and determine if it's connected with the Rocky Mountain Arsonist fires. At least she's okay."

Reid frowned. There had to be a connection here. She was investigating a string of arsons and now she'd come close to dying in a fire?

"Something's off," Reid said. "I need to go back and look inside the house. She told me the door was jammed, and she couldn't get out."

"Apparently, she told the 911 operator that, as well. Did she imply there was something deliberate about this fire?"

"No," Reid said, "but I'd like to look around."

"You always have had good intuition, Reid, but while the fire's finally out, no one's going in there right now. We'll do a full investigation, and in the meantime, why don't you go back into town and check the 911 records of her conversation. Maybe you'll find something there in what she said."

It might have been a long time since he last saw her, but he knew Claire couldn't have changed that much. She'd always been the toughest person he'd ever known. She'd chosen a field that was difficult for men, and even harder for women. Requirements were the same no matter who you were. Lifting heavy equipment, climbing huge ladders and working long shifts, you had to be strong. Strong enough to keep up both physically and emotionally. And yet Claire had excelled, despite the fact that there were few women in her field. The road hadn't always been easy, but her determinedness—

and stubbornness—had pushed her toward the top. He wasn't surprised at all she was now an investigator. That was what she'd always wanted.

But something was definitely wrong.

It was dark when he strode into the sheriff's office where his brother Griffin was on duty at the front desk at half past five.

"Hey…" Griffin got up out of his chair to greet his brother. "I wasn't expecting to see you until dinner tonight at the ranch. Something wrong?"

"It is, actually. You heard about the fire at the B&B?"

"I did. Sounds like the damage is pretty severe, though I was told no one was hurt except for one guest who was trapped in her room and suffered from smoke inhalation."

Reid leaned against the front counter. "That someone was Claire Holiday."

Griffin's eyes widened. "Your Claire Holiday?"

"She's not my Claire, but yes."

"Is she okay?"

"Yes, but it could have been a lot worse."

"What's she doing here?"

"Apparently there are some who believe that the fire at the Reynolds farm might be connected to the Rocky Mountain Arsonist."

"So an arson investigator comes to town and is trapped in a fire?" Griffin frowned. "I'm sorry, but that sounds extremely off to me."

"Yes, it does. I heard they think it might have been started by an electrical fire, but why couldn't she get out? It doesn't make sense. According to her, she was trapped in the room. I know Claire, or at least I used to, and she's not the kind of person to panic in a situation like that. She's trained to know exactly what to do. It just doesn't make sense."

"That does seem to be a pretty odd coincidence. Have you talked to her at all?"

"I'm the one who pulled her out of the fire."

"But have you talked to her?"

"Not really. Just to make sure she was okay."

"I know this has to be awkward for the two of you, but you're probably going to be working with her."

"She'll be working with the captain. Not me."

At least that was his plan.

"I always liked her—"

"Don't even go there." Reid pushed down the rising irritation, knowing exactly where his brother's train of thought was heading. "Just because I'm the last of the O'Callaghan brothers to either be married or engaged, doesn't mean that's going to change."

"That's not what you thought a few years ago."

Reid shoved his hands into his front pockets. "We were different people back then, and I'll be the first to admit that I made a lot of mistakes. I tried to make things right after breaking up with her. She's the one who never responded."

His mother would have called him the prodigal son. She'd told him once that she'd prayed night after night that he'd get his life together, hoping God was working even when she couldn't see it.

Eventually he'd done just that, and never turned back.

"To be fair, you did break up with her," Griffin said.

"I think it's time to drop the subject."

But it was a subject that was hard to forget.

They'd spent their day off skiing in Loveland, then had driven down to Silverthorne where he'd planned a romantic evening at a cozy restaurant. But instead their perfect day had ended in a fight and subsequent break up. Maybe he should have seen it coming. She'd been hinting for weeks that she wanted more out of their relationship. That it was time for them to talk about settling down and getting married. But as much as he'd loved her, back then marriage had terrified him. He just wasn't ready. So instead, he'd panicked and lost her.

"I stopped by because I need your help with something," Reid said, pulling his thoughts out of the past. "I need to listen to the 911 recording of her call."

"That can be arranged. What are you looking for?"

"I'm not sure. I'm hoping I know when I hear it."

A minute later, Griffin had the audio of the call set up at an empty desk. Reid listened to the entire recording, then listened to it a second time.

Ma'am... I'd like you to go try the door again.

I told you it's locked somehow. It won't open.

I understand, but I'd like you to try again. It's easy to panic in a situation like this—

I'm not panicking. It's jammed.

"I don't know." Reid pulled off the headset he'd been wearing, then turned back to his brother. "Something isn't adding up. Claire insists that her door was jammed, as well as the window, and that she couldn't get out. Normally, I'd say it was panic, but she's trained as a firefighter, Griffin. We need to figure out what happened in there."

He didn't want to jump to any conclusions, but what if Claire had been targeted?

TWO

Claire hung up the call with her mom after insisting she was fine and making her mother promise not to tell Owen what had happened. An almost five-year-old didn't need to know that his mom had come close to dying in a fire.

She stared at the gray wall of the emergency room, anxious to leave. She hadn't come to Timber Falls to sit around, and yet the doctor had insisted they observe her for a couple of hours while they checked her oxygen levels. She could feel the exhaustion settling over her body, but the experience had also left her with a sense of restlessness.

She didn't have time to be tired or stuck in an emergency room. She now had two fires to investigate and the sooner she determined exactly what had happened in both cases, the sooner she could get back to Denver.

The fire, though, wasn't the only thing that had shaken her. Reid O'Callaghan had managed to not just walk back into her life, but to save it. She drew in a deep breath and closed her eyes for a moment. It wasn't as if she hadn't expected to see him or his family, because she'd known it was inevitable. Timber Falls was a small town—his hometown—and he was a fireman here. Thinking she could avoid him would have been ignorant. But that didn't change the fact she'd hoped she could have.

Her hands fisted tight on the examination table. The O'Callaghan family had always been the family she'd never had. They'd weathered storms like serious health issues and military deployments by drawing strength from both God and each other. Her own family had never been that way. Stress had pushed her parents apart, eventually leading to a nasty divorce and custody battle. In reality, she knew that no family was perfect, but the O'Callaghans were the family she'd always wanted.

The family she knew now she'd never have.

Reid had made it clear to her the day he broke up with her that he wasn't ready for a wife and family. Forcing a ready-made family on him when she'd found out she was pregnant a few weeks later had been out of the question. Her decision might have kept a son and grandson from the O'Callaghan family, but she'd had no desire to put her son in a similar situation to what she'd been in growing up. Owen had been and always would be her one and only priority.

The sound of footsteps on the tile shifted her attention. She sat up in the bed as Reid stepped through the opening in the curtain carrying a paper bag in his hand. Her heart fought against the reaction that seeing him brought, along with the flash flood of vivid memories. But her relationship with Reid—and any lingering feelings—had been over years ago.

"Hey...am I bothering you?" he asked.

"Reid…no. I… I'm just waiting for the doctor to release me."

And stumbling like a dingbat in front of you.

She sucked in a deep breath of air, willing her pulse to slow down. He still looked just as she remembered. Short, light-brown hair and just a hint of a beard across his face. Fit from working out regularly. She'd always teased him about how he could have made the cover of the firemen's calendar and raised a ton of money for the fire department. He'd always hated the idea, but he was still just as cover-worthy. Today, he was wearing a plaid, fleece-lined jacket, jeans and boots, while looking at her with eyes that had always been able to see all the way inside her.

Eyes that looked just like Owen's.

She tried to shove down the reminder, because Reid finding out the secret she'd kept for close to six years could be almost as devastating as the arsonist she was trying to stop.

He set the bag he was carrying at the end of the bed, clearly feeling just as awkward as she did. "How are you doing?"

"Ready to get out of here. But I'm fine. Nothing more than some smoke inhalation, thanks to you."

"I guess I am the last person you would have imagined coming to your rescue."

"I owe you my life. Thank you."

He shot her a dimpled smile. "You know I was always a sucker for a damsel in distress."

She rolled her eyes at him. "I see you've still got your same sense of humor."

But while his one-liners had always been corny, he was good at his job and she knew it. She just wished he didn't affect her the way he did simply by being in the room with her. After all these years apart, she'd convinced herself she was completely over him and that seeing him again wouldn't matter.

She'd clearly been wrong.

Which meant she was going to have to work harder to ensure the wall around her heart stayed erect and that they didn't spend any more time together than necessary. That shouldn't be very hard, since she'd insist on working with the captain and getting all her information directly from him. All she needed was a couple of days to run her investigation and get evidence from both fires, then she'd go back to Denver. Reid O'Callaghan didn't have to be a part of the equation.

"I'm still trying to put together the pieces of what happened," she said finally, needing to fill the pause between them.

"I listened to your 911 call," he said, "but I thought you could walk me through what happened while it's fresh in your mind."

"Of course." She pulled her legs up under her and tried to organize her thoughts. "I was asleep. I'd gone to bed early, planning to get up early and get to work. The fire alarm woke me. I went to the door, figuring it was just someone who'd gone down to the kitchen in the middle of the night and burnt some toast or something. But I couldn't open the door."

"Like it was locked?" he asked.

"Or jammed somehow. I should have been able to open it from the inside. The knob turned, but the door wouldn't budge."

"Okay."

She cleared her throat. "It didn't take long to realize that the house was on fire. Smoke was coming into my room, so I put a blanket across the threshold. Then I tried the window, but it wouldn't open either. It still makes no sense."

"Panicking would be normal in a situation like that, Claire."

Except she knew that wasn't what had happened.

"You should know me better than that, Reid. I was scared, yes, but I wasn't in a panic. I knew what to do, but the door wouldn't open. The window wouldn't open." She worked to curb the anger in her voice. She needed him to believe her. "Which is why I need to go back now and try to figure out what happened."

"You don't have to convince me. I agree there is something off about the situation."

"You do?"

"Yes." His fingers grasped the metal rail at the end of the bed. "Especially considering the fact that you're trained to be the one doing the rescuing. This time, you were the one trapped in the room—and in the middle of an arson investigation. It's a connection we have to look at. What if the arsonist doesn't want you looking into this?"

"That's exactly what we need to find out." If someone had been behind this fire, that was going to change everything. "And thank you for not just assuming I imagined it."

He let out a low laugh. "You're hardly imagining things. In the meantime, I guess congratulations are in order. I understand you're the fire investigator sent here to check into a recent fire. I always knew you'd go far."

She smiled, thankful for the change in the subject.

"I loved my work as a firefighter, but I love the investigative side even more."

"I've heard you're good at what you do."

She stared up at him, wishing desperately that he didn't still stir her heart like he used to, that she didn't notice the dimple on his chin or the way his hair faded on the sides with a bit of volume on the top. Wishing he wasn't trying to be so…so nice.

"Listen…" She forced the memories aside. "I've been hoping that this won't become…awkward between us."

"Of course not. That's one reason I wanted to see you. First to check on you, but also to clear the air between us. You're here to do a job, and my job is to help you. It won't be a problem."

"Good."

"Just promise me you'll be careful, Claire. No matter how things ended between us in the past, I don't want anything happening to you."

"Thank you. I appreciate that, but I'll be fine."

His concern over her safety didn't surprise her. Even with all that had gone on between them, she remembered that Reid had always been different. He'd opened doors for her and brought her flowers. He'd had this old-fashioned streak that she'd loved. They'd dated for a few months, then she'd met his parents at Christmas here in Timber Falls, always believing she'd marry him.

But then everything had changed.

He'd broken things off with her after a fight and moved back to Timber Falls. Then she'd found out she was pregnant.

A sharp sigh escaped her lips. No. She couldn't let thoughts of Reid interfere with why she was here. Not when she'd finally learned to forget him.

Or, at least, she'd thought she had.

But while he might be just as good-looking and nice as she'd remembered, that didn't matter. Reid was a part of her past, not her future.

Reid shifted his weight at the foot of the bed, feeling awkward, because he'd yet to tell her the real reason he'd come the hospital to see her. And he knew she wasn't going to like it.

He cleared his throat, needing to focus on the situation at hand, prepared for her inevitable reaction. "I came to give you a ride. I can take you back to the B&B fire, but also if you need to go by the store and get anything…"

"I planned on calling an Uber, but thanks. I can manage."

Reid's fingers tightened around the end of the metal bedpost.

"Am I missing something?" Claire asked.

"Sort of."

She frowned. "That wasn't suggestion, was it?"

"The captain asked that I drive you around, just in case there's a connection between the arson fires and what happened at the B&B. He's worried—as I am— that you might have been targeted. At least until we find out what happened, he'd rather be safe than sorry."

He waited for her to argue again, knowing time with him wasn't what she had in mind. She had to have known they were going to run into each other but had planned to make sure she saw him as little as possible. And now they were going to be stuck together—something neither of them wanted.

"So…you're going to be my bodyguard?" she asked.

He shrugged. "That does sound better than a chauffeur, but don't think of it as that. I was on the scene for both fires. If I can't answer any of your questions, I will know who to ask."

"So a bodyguard, chauffer and Siri all rolled into one. I always knew you were talented."

He couldn't help but chuckle. "Funny. You haven't lost your sense of humor either."

She smiled "No, but seriously, I don't need a bodyguard. I'll take an Uber there and hopefully find the keys to my car."

"Humor me, will you? If you don't let me drive you, the captain will be on my back. You don't know how stubborn he can be. I'll even throw in breakfast if you're hungry."

She shot him a grin. "That's quite an offer, but don't think that your charm is going to get me to change my mind."

"Then what about my good looks?"

"You always were incorrigible."

"So we're good?"

Claire let out a sharp sigh. "You can take me there, because you're cheaper than an Uber, but after that, I can drive my own car."

"You'll have to talk with the captain about that. He's meeting us there."

He continued to work to shove the memories of Claire back into the compartment where he'd kept them all these years. Just out of reach, at the edges of his memory, making sure he pushed them back anytime there was a reminder. He'd see that she complied with the captain's orders, then she'd be gone within a few days. And he'd never again have to see the woman who'd once stolen his heart.

The doctor stepped around the curtain, breaking up the awkwardness between them. "Good news. I'm going to let you go home. But if you end up coughing, feeling any shortness of breath or a headache—anything, really, that you think that could have been caused by the fire—I want you to come back in."

"I will," she promised.

"Good. Even without any notable respiratory problems, you can still experience carbon monoxide poisoning. Just be aware of how you're feeling in case something comes up in the next couple days."

Claire swung her legs over the edge of the bed as the doctor left, then stopped and looked down at what she was wearing. "Just one problem. I arrived in these sweats with socks and no shoes."

"I almost forgot. I was able to get you a few things." He handed her the bag he'd brought. "My soon-to-be sister-in-law, Tory, is about your size and offered to let you borrow some clothes until you get yours sorted."

"Wow… I appreciate this so much." Claire dug out the jeans, a long-sleeved Christmas T-shirt, a black cardigan and a pair of boots.

She held up the T-shirt, which depicted a row of plaid Christmas trees.

"Too Christmassy?" Reid asked.

"Can a shirt be too Christmassy?"

Reid shook his head. "You don't want to ask me that, but you'll love Tory."

"Good, and hopefully I'll get to thank her in person. This will really help. It might be a few hours before I can get to my things, and I'd prefer not to smell like smoke that whole time."

"I agree."

"You always did think of everything."

She looked up at him and smiled. Old, familiar feelings shot through him. How was it everything he'd worked to bury all those years ago still had roots? He shoved aside the ridiculous thoughts. Just because Claire was here didn't mean she still had a piece of his heart.

Reid looked up as Shawn Torres, a fellow firefighter, stopped at the edge of the curtain.

"Claire… I hope I'm not interrupting."

"Shawn? No. It's been a long time. It's good to see you."

Reid glanced from Claire to Shawn, then back to Claire again. "You two know each other?"

"We actually went to high school together in Denver," Shawn said. "We've run into each other a few times over the past few years." He turned to Claire. "When I heard your name in connection with the fire…well… I had to come and make sure you're okay."

"I am. Really. Just some smoke inhalation."

Shawn gave her a big hug, then sat down next to her on the bed. "I can't imagine how terrifying that had to be."

"The doctor says I'll be fine. All I want to do now is get this investigation started and see if we can't figure out what's going on."

"I heard someone say you were locked in the room. That doesn't seem coincidental, considering the arson fires you're investigating."

She glanced up at Reid. "News travels fast, doesn't it? I have been thinking the same thing. I'm not sure what happened. The fire alarm went off, but when I tried to get out, the door was jammed. I'm actually planning to head out there now and see what I can find out, though I heard the damage was extensive."

"Sounds like the kitchen and main room are pretty much a total loss, with smoke damage throughout most of the house. Unfortunately, they're going to be closed for a long time. In the meantime, how many days are you planning to be here? It would be nice to reconnect."

"Originally I planned for just two or three, but now... I'm not sure. I need to figure out what happened at both places."

"Are you up for lunch with an old friend? Or maybe a tour of the town? It's beautiful around here, especially this time of year with Christmas around the corner and the snowcapped mountains in the background."

Reid didn't miss the hesitation in Claire's eyes, making him wonder what she was thinking. Or maybe he was imagining things and it was nothing more than fatigue.

"Let me see how things go before I commit to anything, but I'd like that."

"And in the meantime," Shawn said, "I'd be happy to drive you anywhere you need to go."

"That's sweet of you, but the captain has already arranged something for me. Apparently Reid is now my chauffeur. At least until I can get things sorted on my end."

"Sounds good." Shawn stood up and nodded. "Looks like everything is working out, but if you do need anything, you have my number. Don't hesitate to call."

"I won't, and thank you, Shawn. I appreciate it."

"Sounds like the two of you go way back," Reid said after Shawn had left the room.

"We do. He's always been a good friend."

"He's a good fireman, as well."

"I'm going to need a few minutes to get dressed and check out of here."

Reid cleared his throat. "No hurry. I need to grab something back at my house, then I'll meet you right outside the front doors."

Reid closed the curtain behind him, then headed outside to his truck. He wasn't jealous of Shawn. No. That would be ridiculous. Shawn might have a history with Claire, but so did Reid, and there was nothing between the two of them anymore. Whatever they'd had was long over and there was no going back. She was going to do her job and uncover who was behind these fires, and then she'd step out of his life again forever.

THREE

Claire headed out the front door of the small hospital and breathed in the fresh mountain air. Despite everything that had happened, she was grateful to be alive. A gray, double-cab truck pulled up, and Reid jumped out of the driver's seat.

"I see you've got your same old truck," she said, stopping in front of him.

"You know me. Not sure I'll ever be able to give her up. But before we leave, I want you to meet someone."

Her brow furrowed. "Okay."

She followed him to the backseat of the truck, then waited for him to open the door.

"This is Sasha." He undid the car harness, then gave the command for the German shepherd to jump down and sit. "I'm in the process of training her to work as an arson dog."

"Wow. She's gorgeous."

Claire knelt down in front of the dog and scratched her behind her ears.

"And smart. She can pick up the scent of fire starters and accelerants, and is already earning her keep." Reid let out a low laugh. "And all she wants in return is some food, a bit of tug-of-war with her favorite toy and a lot of love."

Sasha nuzzled her face against Claire. "That can't be too hard to give her."

"Not at all. I think she likes you."

"Well, I definitely like her too. How did you learn to train her?"

"I took some classes in Denver as well as online. It's been a boost for our department and something I really enjoy."

"You're a beautiful girl. Yes, you are," Claire said, stroking the dog's head.

Claire stood up as Reid commanded Sasha to get back into the truck, then hooked her into her harness.

"You ready to head to the B&B?"

"I am."

Claire slipped into the passenger seat, unable to suppress the memories of Reid and this town as Reid pulled out of the parking lot and headed south on the main road. Timber Falls had that small-town feel and yet it was still large enough for there to be plenty to do. Tourists loved the nearby skiing, the quaint bed-and-breakfasts scattered along the town's edges, and the outdoor activities and shopping. Locals loved waking up to a spectacular view and the opportunity to breathe in clean mountain air every morning.

As for the entire O'Callaghan family…at one time she'd imagined being a part of it. Jacob and Marci O'Callaghan owned a stunning ranch that had been in the family since the early nineteen hundreds. The ranch itself was beautiful with views of Pikes Peak and the surrounding mountains.

"You okay?"

She shifted her attention back to Reid. "Sorry, I've forgotten just how beautiful it is down here. It's been too long since I visited."

"I know. I never tire of the views."

They'd spent time here hiking, fly-fishing and even hunting for turkey, so she could get to know his family. But that seemed so long ago.

Still, she glanced at his profile, wondering if she affected him as much as he was affecting her right now. No matter how hard she tried, his presence made forgetting all those memories impossible.

"My offer for breakfast is still good," he said, interrupting her thoughts. "You have to be hungry."

"I'm fine, but thank you. Someone brought me coffee earlier at the hospital."

"That's not breakfast."

"How is your mom?" Claire asked, changing the subject.

"My mom… She's good. She wasn't working today, but she's still at the medical center three or four days a week, and she helps my dad at the ranch the rest of the time."

"And your brothers? It's been so long since I've seen your family."

As an only child, she'd loved hanging out with him and his three brothers, and had been a little jealous of their close relationships. Their life had always seemed ideal to her.

"Let's see," he said. "A lot has happened since you were here. Liam's married with two adorable children. He's in the army and is being transferred to Fort Hood after Christmas. My mom isn't happy about that, as you can imagine, after having her only grandbabies so close, but I have a feeling she'll be going down there quite a bit."

Claire stared out the window as another wave of guilt struck. She'd always tried not to think about how her decision had affected more people than just Reid.

"And Griffin?" she asked, forcing her voice to stay even. "I understand he's a deputy?"

"He is. He's getting married in a couple weeks to Tory, who works at the medical center. They bought a cabin on an acre of land up Lincoln Road last month and are blissfully happy. His words, not mine."

"A Christmas wedding." Claire laughed. "I bet it will be beautiful."

She breathed in slowly, thankful that some of the tension had eased between them, though maybe it was just the shift in the conversation. Reid had always loved his brothers and talking about his family. And she'd loved hanging out with them, as well.

"My brother Caden is recently engaged to Gwen. They're working together to create an equine-assisted therapy program at the ranch."

"Wow…that sounds wonderful," she said. "And you're right. Lots of changes. What about you?"

"What about me?"

"Married…girlfriend?"

He let out a low laugh. "I date some, but I've pretty much come to the conclusion that settling down and having a family isn't in my future. Which is fine. I love my job, live near family, have some great friends and there's Sasha…"

Reid kept talking, but she only heard one thing.

Settling down and having a family isn't in my future.

Her jaw tensed. Clearly she'd made the right decision all those years ago, after all.

"What about you?"

His question yanked her back to the present. She was going to have to find a way to stay more focused around him. "Sorry?"

"Are you in a relationship?"

"Me? No. My job and other responsibilities keep me busy."

"I'm surprised someone hasn't snatched you up. Anyway, I almost forgot something else. My mother called me when she found out you were in town."

"Once again, word travels fast."

Reid chuckled as he pulled off the main road and into the driveway of the B&B. "She…she wanted to know if you had any plans tonight, and if I don't invite you…"

Claire's fingers clutched the armrest as Reid guided the truck down the long drive. "I don't know, Reid—"

At least the invite wasn't coming from Reid. But while she didn't want to hurt his mom's feelings, Claire wasn't sure this was a good idea. She'd come to Timber Falls knowing that seeing Reid was unavoidable, but she'd convinced herself she could put the past behind her and just focus on her job. He might have been a distraction in the past, but things were different now. They'd parted ways, and in a few days she'd be gone again. She took in a deep breath and pushed away the regrets and guilt.

"You really don't have to come," Reid said.

"No. I'd love to see your family."

She'd go for an hour or two, feign a headache, then leave. Seeing his family was something she'd have to do at some point. She might as well get it over with.

"Great…then it's settled."

"Great."

"I can drive you there."

"I have a car. And I remember my way."

"Maybe, but you'll have to clear that with the captain first."

"Don't worry. I will."

There was no way she was going to have Reid pick her up and make this look like a date. She was only going because she'd always liked and respected his parents and it had been so long since she'd seen them.

She'd thought they were going to be her in-laws one day.

She'd imagined being Reid's wife. Then everything had changed. He'd broken up with her, telling her he wasn't interested in settling down. Then she'd found out she was pregnant.

And she'd never told him the truth.

She squashed the train of thought. A reunion with Reid's family wasn't why she was here, and something told her she was going to regret her decision to see them.

She looked back at him, then caught the worried lines on Reid's face as he glanced in the rearview mirror.

"Reid… What's wrong?"

His hands gripped the steering wheel. "We're being tailgated."

"Tailgated?"

She glanced behind her and saw a white, single cab pickup following inches behind their bumper. Adrenaline shot through her as she grabbed automatically for the dashboard. A smaller car could easily be clipped and sent into a fishtail in a situation like this, but even in Reid's double-cab truck this was a dangerous situation. What was the other driver thinking? The narrow, two-lane road curved in front of them, and the other vehicle wasn't slowing down.

"Do you recognize the vehicle?" she asked.

"No."

"If they're in a hurry, why don't they just go around us?" She zoomed in on the windshield and the driver. "I can't see their face. They're wearing a hat and sunglasses."

Why would someone want to run them off the road?

Panic pressed against her chest. She wanted to dismiss the thought before it germinated, but it was already too late. What if this was somehow related to the fire at the B&B? What if someone really did want her out of the way?

"Hang on." Reid pushed his foot on the accelerator as he took another curve, but the second truck simply sped up, staying on their tail.

"I should be able to slow down and let them pass," he said, "but it doesn't matter what I do. He won't go around me."

"Should I call 911?" she asked, grabbing for her phone out of her purse that was on the floorboard.

The truck's tires squealed.

Reid tapped on his breaks.

"Wait a minute. Looks like they're going to pass." Reid slowed down as the truck flew past them. "Can you read the license?"

She strained to see. "Looks like it's muddied out."

Reid drove another quarter of a mile, then pulled off the road in a safe place and put the truck in Park. "You okay?"

"A little shaken, but yeah."

"What about you, girl?" He turned around and rubbed Sasha behind the ears.

"That was some good driving back there," Claire said. "I wasn't sure you were going to make that last curve at that speed."

He let out a huff of air. "You and me both."

"Someone was in a hurry."

"I don't know. That seemed like more than a bad day. It seemed almost—"

"Personal?" She shook her head. "That was my first thought, but I think the fire has my imagination working overtime. I could be wrong, but I'd rather stick to that theory."

Because the alternative terrified her.

Ten minutes later, Reid pulled up in front of the B&B, still trying to process what had just happened on the road. He'd thought about calling Griffin and report the tailgating incident, but decided Claire was probably right. It was just someone who'd had a bad day and was in a hurry. They had more important things to deal with today than a bad driver.

Once they confirmed it was safe to enter the B&B, Reid headed with Claire and Sasha toward the second-story room where she'd slept last night.

The strong smell of smoke permeated the house, and the damage was extensive on the first floor, which was heartbreaking. The B&B had become a popular place to stay for tourists looking for a mountain getaway and some home cooking.

The blackened walls of the kitchen—where the fire had been the worst—showed just how damaging the flames had been. They'd devoured anything flammable, including the Christmas tree and decorations, and melted almost everything else. The upstairs had received less damage, but it was still going to take time to reconstruct what had been ruined.

"I'm thankful no one was hurt," he said as they took the stairs, "but this is so sad. The Grahams have owned this place for decades."

"I was thinking the same thing."

Claire stopped just inside the open door of her room and studied the interior. Even though the flames hadn't reached inside, the smoke had caused discoloration along the walls and surfaces, and the smell of it still lingered in the air.

"I'll do a thorough investigation of the entire house," she said. "But first… I need to understand what happened here. Why I couldn't get out."

Sasha sat next to Reid as Claire started going through the room, beginning with the door and ending with the window. She didn't say anything as she assessed the scene, focusing instead entirely on the job at hand. He watched her work, not surprised at how seriously she took her job, her expression intense as she combed the room for clues.

"Do you see anything that stands out?" he asked as she turned back to him.

"There's some debris in the window's sliding track as well as some rust that has accumulated. But there doesn't seem to be any obvious sign of tampering. And while I thought I checked it last night, I was pretty tired when I got in and probably didn't. But the door…" She turned back around to him. "It doesn't make sense that the door wouldn't open."

"I believe you, if that means anything. I had to break down the door."

"But why?"

He knew she was searching for something to prove that all of this was nothing more than an electrical fire, and for whatever reason, the door had swelled and stuck from the heat of the fire.

"It's possible that the door stuck because of swelling," he said, "or because the handle was old and the locking mechanism stuck."

"Maybe."

She stood in front of the window again, going over every inch of the frame. Watching her work, no matter how hard he tried, he couldn't escape the memories or the details of their relationship. Like how her favorite food was grilled cheese sandwiches. How she loved to swim and had once considered competing on a national level and trying to make it into the Olympics. How she loved daisies and walking in the rain.

For almost six years, Reid had tried to forget her, and most of the time he succeeded. But then he'd dream about her, and it always seemed so real, he could almost smell her perfume lingering in the air when he woke up. But despite calling her dozens of times, he'd never seen her again after the day he'd broken things off with her. Eventually, he'd done his best to put her out of his mind. He'd tried dating again, but for some reason, no one had made him feel the way Claire did.

Which is why he'd told her he couldn't see himself settling down and having a family. Even all these years later, she was the only person he'd ever been able to imagine being with.

"Reid."

"Sorry… I was thinking of something else."

Of you.

Something he had to stop.

Having her back in town and working with her meant too many memories were swirling on the surface, and he couldn't quite figure out how to stuff them back into the box where he'd had them locked away for so long.

But he'd made too many mistakes with Claire, and he had no desire to rekindle a relationship that was based on the person he used to be. Back then, he'd bought into the lie that he was too far gone for God to forgive the constant string of bad choices he'd made. Instead, he went to bed guilty at night when he'd drunk too much or partied too hard, because it was easier to just sweep it under the table and cover it up in the darkness.

But looking back he'd realized that God had never stopped working.

"I was just wondering if you had any theories," she said, breaking into his thoughts.

"Not yet. Tell me about the arson fires you've been working on," he said, shifting his train of thought.

"The arsonist has always used an accelerant, as well as a slow-burning device. We also always found an antique lighter at the scene—like they were a part of someone's collection. We're still working to trace them, but so far haven't been able to."

"I'll be honest," Reid said. "I haven't really heard much about the fires."

"That's been on purpose. We've tried to keep the connections away from any news outlets, since many arsonists love the attention and it often fuels the fires. We need to avoid that."

"The farm building that burned down last week… that's the reason you're here."

She nodded.

"Who knows you're here?" he asked.

"It's not like it's been announced. I haven't told anyone except my mother, and of course my boss knows and your captain." She rested her hands on her hips. "Can you have Sasha search the house for any accelerant?"

"Of course."

"I think if we do find some, it will be downstairs, but it's worth looking here too. Our arsonist's MO has been acetone and gasoline."

Reid gave Sasha the command, then followed as she made her way around the room.

Nothing.

He bent down and rubbed her behind the ears. "Good girl, Sasha."

"Why don't we take her downstairs and see if she can find something," Claire said.

"Claire Holiday…" Captain Ryder stepped into the room and held out his hand to shake Claire's. "I'm sorry I didn't make it to the hospital to check on you, but I'm glad you're here."

"Reid's been taking good care of me."

"I knew he would. I apologize for the rocky welcome. This fire…are you okay?"

"I'm fine. I just want to get to the bottom of this as soon as possible."

"I spoke to the owners. Mr. Graham said the window does have a habit of getting stuck, but no one has ever complained about the door."

"A possible coincidence then?" she asked.

"Perhaps, but you need to see this." Captain Ryder pulled an evidence bag out of his pocket. "We found this antique brass lighter downstairs in the preliminary scene assessment. The Grahams said it wasn't theirs. I understand it fits into the arsonist's MO."

"It does." Claire's face paled as she caught Reid's gaze. "Which indicates that what happened here has to be connected to the Rocky Mountain fires."

A wave of nausea swept through Reid. "And it's further proof that your being locked in this room wasn't an accident."

FOUR

Claire stood in the middle of the room where she'd slept the night before, struggling to process their theory about the fire. The fact that there had been no accelerant in the bedroom didn't surprise her. There would have been far more damage. The finding of the lighter confirmed that this was connected to the arsonist she was searching for. This brought the total up to ten fires and added thousands of dollars more in damages. At least no one had died this time.

Sunlight filtered through the white lace curtains, leaving patches of light across the rug. The only thing that remained of the fire was the heavy scent of smoke still lingering in the room, but if the fire department hadn't put out the fire as quickly as they had, the entire house could have been destroyed.

She turned in a slow circle, taking in the details of the room, not really sure what she was looking for. Had someone really tried to lock her in the room? Or were they jumping to conclusions too early with the limited evidence they had?

She held up the evidence bag from the captain and studied the antique brass lighter. Without this, she might have been able to convince herself that this fire was simply a coincidence. The house was old, the wiring possibly faulty. She could also explain away the supposed jammed door, as well. Wood swelled at certain times of the year and old houses were known for their list of issues. A stuck door or window wasn't uncommon. Everything that had happened could be explained away by the fact that she'd just been in the wrong place at the wrong time.

But the lighter she was holding told a completely different story. She might believe in coincidences, but this was too much to be an accident. There had to be a connection between this fire and the arsons she was investigating, but did that mean she'd been targeted?

"Claire...what are you thinking?"

She looked at Reid and caught the concern in his eyes. "We're going to have to move forward with the assumption that this is connected to the string of arson fires I'm investigating."

"I think you're right," Reid said.

"Is the scene secure?" she asked.

"It is," the captain said.

"But you don't have to be the one doing the investigating," Reid said. "Someone else can come in, because if you're a target—"

"One, I'm still not sure if I am a target, and two, even if I am, I'm the perfect person to continue working this case." She handed the captain back the lighter, certain she was making the right decision. "I investigated the other fires, which means I know firsthand the signature of the arsonist and what to look for better than anyone else. This is my investigation, and I'm going to see it through. We need to stop whoever's behind it."

"Yes, we do," Reid said. "I'm just concerned that—"

"I'll be fine, Reid." She held up her hand as if waving away his concerns. "And something tells me I'll have plenty of security ensuring my safety."

"She's right," the captain said. "Not only do I want you to continue as the liaison for our department, Reid, but to also keep an eye on her. I've already spoken to the sheriff's department, and they're going to be on high alert for anything suspicious going on in and around town. They've also promised to double their presence wherever you end up staying, Claire. You can call them day or night and they'll be there immediately."

Claire let out a sigh, knowing that there was no use arguing with either of them. "I appreciate the concern, even though I'm not convinced it's necessary. In the meantime, we need to get moving on this investigation. I want to do a scene assessment, starting with the origin of the fire, in order to ensure that the scene has been documented with both video and photos, and I want the photos printed out."

The captain nodded. "Not a problem. The sheriff's also doing interviews with all the guests and will give us that information as soon as he's done."

"Perfect. Just let him know I might need to do follow-up interviews."

"Of course."

She turned to Reid. "I'd like Sasha to see if she can detect any accelerant downstairs."

Claire followed the men out of the room, stopping only to pick up a penny wedged next to the door at the edge of the carpet. She was going to treat this like any other suspicious fire. She'd do her job evaluating and processing the scene and the evidence thoroughly, as always, and find whoever was behind the fires, making sure he never did something like this again.

Downstairs, the kitchen walls were blackened, and the intense smell of smoke lingered in the air.

"It's sad," she said, while Reid and Sasha searched for signs of accelerant. "This was such a beautiful place, and it's going to take a lot of time to restore things. What did you find?"

The captain stopped in front of one of the walls next to her. "Both the burn pattern and the blistering of the wood points to this being where the fire originated. On the surface it looks like an electrical issue might have started it. We found an aluminum wire connected to a copper switch, which could have caused a short."

"Maybe." Claire studied the patterns of fire that had become familiar over the years. It was almost like reading the pages of a book. "We need to know if this area tests positive for an accelerant. The alligator char doesn't always mean that a liquid accelerant was present."

"This time it does," Reid said, crouching next to Sasha, who was sitting with a proud look on her face.

"I don't smell anything," she said, walking over to them.

"It's there. Trust me."

She started sifting through the debris until she was able to pull up a small piece of the subflooring. She took a whiff. "Your girl was right. It smells like gasoline. So an accelerant was definitely used."

She stood back up, studying the room. "Where did you find the lighter, captain?"

"On the other side of the kitchen. Next to the stove." The captain crossed the room and pointed to the spot.

Ten fires now, in the past eighteen months. The targets had been everything from commercial property to private homes. Always an antique lighter found near the origin of the fire. Some had been melted from the heat, but all had been identified as lighters.

"What do you know about these vintage lighters?" Reid asked.

"They used to be as common on people as cell phones are today," she said. "We're trying to track them down, but the problem is that you can buy them anywhere online today."

"Which means narrowing it down is going to be like trying to find a needle in a haystack," Reid said.

"Exactly." Claire took a step back then turned to the captain. "While your team gets the photos together and you work on your initial assessment, I'd like to speak to the owners."

"Of course. They're outside working in their garden, hoping to be able to go through the house and see what they can salvage. I told them they'd have to wait until we could give them the go-ahead."

"Good call."

The captain nodded toward the front door. "Why don't the two of you go talk with them while we finish up here."

Mike and Sarah Graham, the owners of the B&B, were out working in their rose garden, which had been spared from the fire.

"I bet these are stunning when they're all in bloom," Claire said, stopping in the middle of the manicured section.

Sarah stood and pulled off her garden gloves before petting Sasha. "What a beautiful dog. And you're right, the garden is stunning. The temperatures are supposed to drop down into the twenties tonight. I'd planned to work today on mulching them to protect them from the cold, but now… I'm not sure it matters. If we don't have a B&B come spring, who's going to care if my roses are thriving?"

"I know this must all seem overwhelming," Reid said, "but you'll rebuild and reopen again. Just give yourselves some time."

"I hope so." Her husband set the shovel he was using against the tree and joined them. "Honestly, we're just thankful no one was injured. It could have been so much worse. We heard…" Mike glanced at his wife. "We heard you had a problem with the door to your room being jammed when the fire alarm was going off. If anything had happened to you or any of the guests—"

Claire shook her head. "I want you both to stop feeling guilty over what happened. I'm all right. Everyone who was here is all right, and that's what really matters. You're going to have enough on your plate to get things rebuilt. Let me assure you, I've seen dozens of fires in my career, and you will be able to rebuild and open up again. Like Reid said, you are just going to have to give yourselves some time."

"I'm trying to remember that." Sarah dropped her hands to her sides as she blinked back tears. "We've worked so hard to get this place up and running, and just when thing were going well… I don't know. Starting over just seems so overwhelming."

"I'm sure it's easy to think about closing after something like this," Claire said, "but don't make any decisions yet. And in the meantime, we need to ask you a couple questions."

"Of course."

"Did you hear anything or see anything out of place during the night?" Claire asked.

Sarah glanced at her husband. "I wish I could say yes, but I normally sleep like a rock and I did last night. Mike? Anything?"

"I did get up in the night, actually. I thought I heard one of the guests downstairs, maybe getting something to eat. Sarah always leaves out a few snacks in the dining room in case someone can't sleep."

"And when you went downstairs, did you see anyone?" Reid asked.

"No. No one was there."

"So what did you do?" Claire asked.

"I checked the back door, which was unlocked. That was odd, as well."

"Do you normally lock up the house?"

"Always. I thought it was possible someone went outside because they forgot something in their car, but when I went outside to check, no one was there."

"How long was that before the fire?"

"Not long, actually. I locked the back door, then went back upstairs and had just fallen asleep again when the fire alarm went off."

"And when you were downstairs, before the fire. Did you smell any smoke?"

"No, but honestly, I don't have a very sensitive nose, so I probably wouldn't have noticed."

"Do you have any security cameras set up?" Claire said.

"We have cameras on the front and back doors. Despite the fire, there's a good chance we can download the footage."

"Good," Claire said. "Is there anything else you can think of? Anything out of the ordinary that might have happened the last couple days?"

"I can't think of anything," Mike said.

"No. Me neither." Sarah glanced at her husband for a moment, then turned back to Claire. "Are you thinking this wasn't just an electrical fire?"

"That's what we're going to find out. We will need access to your security footage."

"Of course. Anything you want," Sarah said.

"I appreciate it," Claire said. "And in the meantime, don't worry. You have enough on your plate. You should be able to get back into the house soon, and please let us know if you think of anything else that might help."

"We will."

Claire followed Reid down the stone path back to the house, her mind processing the information they'd just been given.

"I think the arsonist was in the house, not someone coming down to get something to eat," she said. "And then he slipped outside to avoid getting caught."

"I think you're right."

"We need to go look at that security footage and see if we can identify who was in the house as well as anyone who showed up at the scene."

Reid set a paper sack down in front of Claire, along with an orange juice for her and a coffee for him, then took a seat next to her in front of the computer where she'd been going through security footage from the B&B in the conference room of the sheriff's office. "Find anything yet?"

"No, but it looks like you did." Claire shot him a huge grin. "Don't tell me you went by Fiona's."

"I told you I was going to go grab something, and if I remember correctly, you used to love sausage biscuits for breakfast."

She smiled at him. "And I still do."

"Good. Because Fiona still makes the best biscuits in town."

"You're doing a good job of reminding me of everything I loved about this place." Claire opened the bag and took in a deep breath. "You know exactly how to make me feel nostalgic. I don't think much has changed in this town since I was here last."

"I don't know about that. The mayor just had all the streetlights downtown replaced."

She let out a soft chuckle. "Like I said, not much has changed."

"How are you feeling?" he asked as she unloaded the bag and split the food between them.

"Are you speaking to me as a friend or my bodyguard?"

"It is my job to make sure you're okay."

She caught his gaze and frowned. "I'm fine, Reid."

"Just following the doctor's suggestions. Any coughing…shortness of breath…headache?"

"No. No. And…no."

"Good."

"But…" she prompted. "I know there's going to be a *but* in there somewhere."

"I might still think you should bring in someone else to take over the case so you can take the next few days off and rest."

She took a bite of the sausage biscuit, ignoring him for the moment.

"Claire."

She shook her head. "Do you really think I'll be able to rest after what happened? Just sit around for the weekend, twiddling my thumbs and wondering what's going on down here? If you do, then you don't remember how determined I can be."

"Okay." He held up his hands in defeat and laughed, but his smile quickly faded. "I just know how close you came to succumbing to those fumes."

"I'll concede to one thing," she said. "I could have lost my life last night and that isn't something I'm taking lightly. I promise. But neither am I ready to simply walk away. I've been working on this case for six months, ever since I made the connection between the fires. I know it better than anyone else, which is why I'm determined not to just walk away. You have to understand that. Two men are dead, and I could have been a third victim. We have to find this guy."

Reid grabbed his breakfast sandwich and started to unwrap it. "You know, you haven't changed at all, and yes, I do remember how stubborn, I mean, determined you can be."

"I suggest you tread carefully, Reid O'Callaghan." Her tone was serious, but she was still smiling.

"All I'm saying is that not only were you always good at whatever you did, you were never one to simply walk away when things got hard. It was one of the things I used to love about you." Reid felt his jaw tense, realizing he'd trod smack dab into the middle of a minefield. He did not need to be flirting with her. "I'm sorry…that didn't come out the way I intended. I meant—"

"Forget it." She took a sip of her orange juice, not missing a beat. "I know what you meant, and I appreciate it. Really. But let's try to avoid any awkwardness between us. *We* were a long time ago. And I'd like to think that we are both professional enough to do our jobs without letting the past get in the way. And even that maybe we could be friends again."

"I'd like that."

"Me too."

But just friends had never been a part of their relationship.

He took a bite of his sausage biscuit, then washed it down with some coffee. "So tell me, did you find anything else in the footage while I was gone?"

"Unfortunately, no."

A knock on the door drew Reid's attention behind them.

"Shawn…" Claire rolled her chair back a couple of inches.

"Sorry to interrupt. The captain asked me to print out some still shots from the security footage from the night of the fire for you, including a few spectators who showed up at the scene."

"Perfect. Thank you so much."

"Of course." Shawn set a manila envelope on the desk. "Is there anything else you need? I could help you go over them if you need an extra eye."

"I think Reid and I have it covered at the moment, but this is going to help. A lot."

"I hope so. I still can't get over how close that fire came to destroying that house." Shawn shoved his hands into his back pockets. "Anyway, if you don't need anything, then I'll leave you to it."

"Sounds good. And thanks again, Shawn." After he left the room, Claire reached for her orange juice and took another sip. "Want to go over these with me?"

"You know I need to be useful. I have no desire to simply be a bodyguard."

Claire laughed as she spread out the photos in front of her. "We are inside the sheriff's office, so I feel pretty safe."

"That was the point. You're staying safe. If you're a target in this, we can't let this guy get close to you again."

"I agree, though don't think you can keep me here indefinitely. I still need to go see the site of the other fire."

"We've got photos of that fire, as well."

"Good try. For now, though, let's try to identify everyone in these photos."

"I can probably do that pretty easily for you." Reid grabbed one of the photos. "Looks like most of these are neighbors and familiar faces. For instance, this is Carly Bridges. She lives next door to the Grahams."

"Perfect. I'll start a list of names we know, and then we'll flag any you might not know."

Reid held up a different photo. "Sid Benson lives across the street. He used to work for the post office, but retired about a year ago. Spends most of his time growing orchids in his greenhouse and visiting his kids in Denver."

"Also sounds like an unlikely suspect."

"Agreed," He pointed to another photo. "I'm not sure who this couple is."

"I am. They were guests of the B&B. Flew in from Virginia two nights ago for a long weekend in the mountains."

"So we can cross them off the list, as well."

"Look at this guy, behind them." Claire tapped on the photo. "He's in the back of the crowd, and he's wearing a hoodie. Does he look familiar?"

"No… I've never seen him before."

"I think I have."

"Where?"

"One of the other fires." She pulled up a separate file on her computer, then clicked through some photos until she stopped at one and enlarged it. "It's hard to tell, but look in the back, left corner. Seems about the same height, same hair color and a possible tattoo on his left hand."

Reid let out a sharp huff of air. "The resolution is a bit blurry, but I think you might be right."

"Then we need to go through all the photos again and see if we can find a clearer one. We need a positive ID on this guy."

"Is it as beautiful as you remember?" he asked, as they headed for the barn.

"Even more so," she said, willing her mind to focus on the landscape that still had patches of snow from the last storm left in the shadows beneath evergreen trees.

"Sounds like you need to get out of the city more."

Claire breathed in mountain air. "You're right. I probably should. Everything is just so…busy. It's hard to find time."

"That's why I don't think I'd ever leave here again. It's as if life has slowed down a few paces from the rest of the world out here, and I can't imagine trading that for traffic jams and all the noise."

"It has its benefits, though. When's the last time you had street tacos from that food truck we used to eat at or went to the theater?"

"You do have a point."

She laughed, trying to let herself ease the tension between them some. Still, he was close enough that she could smell his familiar cologne and see the gold flecks in his eyes when he looked at her. Which shouldn't matter. She'd worked too long to guard her heart against him. In another couple of days, she'd be back to her life where things were predictable and she didn't have to worry about running into Reid O'Callaghan. The way it should be.

Ten minutes later she was wearing a pair of cowboy boots, and they were saddled up on two mares and heading toward the trail they always used to take to the lake. Reid was right about one thing—she did need to get out of the city more, especially with Owen. They went hiking occasionally, but there was something about being

here, in the middle of God's creation, that helped tug away the layers of stress that had been pressing on her.

"I wanted to apologize," he said, glancing at her.

She tightened her grip on the reins. "Apologize? For what?"

"You are perfectly capable of doing your job, and I might have come across a bit…"

"Overprotective."

"I was thinking simply protective, but yes. You can say overprotective. You've worked hard to get where you are, and I don't ever want you to think that just because—"

"I'm a woman?"

"Putting words into my mouth again?"

She pressed her lips together. "I tend to speak too much when I'm nervous."

"I remember." He shot her a smile. "And for the record, you're not just any woman, as far as I'm concerned. Our history might have ended years ago, but that doesn't mean I don't think about you, hoping you're doing okay. Are you happy?"

"I am," she said, surprised at his question. "I live close to my mom and see her a lot. I enjoy my job. Life is good."

"And you're still okay about seeing my family tonight? It's bound to be a bit chaotic. You remember how my brothers were, and now with the family growing… I just don't want you to be overwhelmed."

"I'll be fine, and besides, it will be nice to catch up. I've missed your parents and will enjoy the fact that there's finally a few more women in the mix."

"I'm pretty sure my mom enjoys that too."

Claire kept her eyes focused on the horizon where

the sun had begun its drop behind the mountains. Soon the temperature would fall, but for now, the crisp air felt perfect. Being here was only for tonight. She could handle that. They'd share a few old stories, laugh and then she'd go back to her world where Reid was nothing more than a distant memory. A place where he needed to stay.

"How long do you think you'll be in town?" he asked.

"Just until I can get some answers about this case. I feel like I'm always one step behind in finding our arsonist."

"Tomorrow's another day. We can go out to the Reynolds farm tomorrow so you can see that scene, though I know you have all the photographs of it."

"I'd still like to see it in person."

"Can I give you some advice?" he asked.

"Okay."

"Forget about the case for the moment and enjoy the view."

He was right. She pulled slightly on the reins to slow down the gait of the horse, wanting to slow down time for a moment. It had been too long since she'd enjoyed scenery like this. The sun cast streaks of yellow and orange across the horizon and filtered down across the lake in front of them.

"Wow…this is still so stunning. It's as if nothing has changed in all the years since I've been here."

"I remember how much you loved this spot."

She felt her hands tremble against the reins. He remembered too many things about her.

Reid leaned over to steady his horse, which had suddenly become agitated.

"Reid…what's wrong?"

"I don't know." He started turning the horse in a slow circle. "Did you hear that?"

"Hear what?"

"It sounds like bees."

She could hear it now, and smelled a tinge of smoke in the air. A streak of orange shot out in front of Reid, jerking her attention back to the left.

"Reid…"

"Head to the tree line. Now. It's some kind of drone."

A drone?

Whatever it was, it was shooting fire at them.

She tugged on the reins and tried to steer her horse away from the potential danger out in the open. Fire-fighters often used drones to show heat signatures, locate a victim in a fire or even determine exactly where the fire was. Flame-throwing drones could be used to clear power lines and agriculture burns. But this…this was clearly an attack.

She could hear the crackle of the flames as the drone shot out another long stream of fire behind her, this time hitting inches to the left of Reid. Orange flames crackled behind her. A row of bushes caught fire.

"Whoa, boy…you're okay." She worked to calm down her own agitated horse, while trying to keep her balance on the saddle as she studied the scene, now from the tree line.

The buzzing drone swooped down again as Reid raced toward her. Another ball of flames shot out from the spider-like contraption. A second later, Reid lost his grip and was thrown off his horse.

Reid hit the ground with a hard thud at the edge to the clearing, then moaned as his horse galloped away.

He fought to catch his breath, then tried to sit up. Something was wrong. The buzzing sound of the drone had been replaced by the hissing noise of a fire. And that terrified him more than the flame-spitting robot. While winter weather tended to put an end to wildfires, snowfall didn't completely eliminate the threat. And a fire out of control would devastate the ranch.

"Reid…" Claire slid off her horse a dozen feet from him.

"I'm okay. Get that fire out."

She secured the reins to a tree and ran toward the fire spreading across a pile of dry brush. By the time he managed to stand up, she'd doused the small fire with fresh snow. If this had been summertime, things could have ended differently. All it took was a few sparks and a whole section of the ranch could have been on fire. But a flame-shooting drone? Why would anyone do that?

"What about the drone?" he asked, brushing off his pants legs.

"It's gone."

Reid frowned. It might be gone for now, but someone had been behind the attack. He took a step and felt his leg give way. She ran toward him and grabbed onto his arm, ensuring he stayed upright. He was going to be sore tomorrow.

"Are you sure you're okay?" she asked, searching his expression. "Nothing broken?"

"I don't think so. Just a few bruises."

She grasped his hand and turned it over. "You've got a burn."

"It's just a singe," he argued.

"At least I know now you're still both tough *and* stubborn."

Reid shrugged. "I figure I wouldn't be much of a bodyguard if I'm injured. Unless you're trying to get rid of me."

Her laugh eased the tension hanging in the air but couldn't erase the seriousness of the situation. Still...

He couldn't help but smile back at her. "Though this is a new one for the books."

She let go of his hand, no longer any sign of a smile on her lips. "You know this was no coincidence."

"Yes, but why? Why come at me with some...some fire-breathing drone? We know that whoever was flying that drone could see exactly what was happening. They shot those flames precisely where they wanted them to land. They weren't coming for you this time."

She shook her head. "I agree, but I don't know why."

"Me neither, though what I do know is that it's going to be dark soon. We need to get back to the house."

"And we need to go talk to Griffin."

"Yes, but I also need to find my horse. More than likely she didn't go far."

She glanced at her horse, still tied to the tree. "Care for a ride?"

"Yeah...that would be great."

He managed to get up onto the horse, then pulled her up behind him. She started to put her arms around his waist, then pulled away.

"I'm sorry."

"It's fine. Really."

He felt her arms wrap back around him as they headed in the direction the horse had gone while the sun continued to drop deeper into the horizon. A part of him wished she wasn't so close, while another part

of him—his heart—wanted to turn around and kiss her like he hadn't done for years.

"I see her up ahead. You were right. She didn't go far."

Her statement pulled him back into the present where he should be—not lost in a pile of broken dreams. He studied the tree line and saw the mare standing in the shadows.

He got down off the horse, then helped Claire, ignoring her closeness as her hair brushed his shoulder.

"Can you ride her back to the house?" she asked.

"I think she'll be fine. She's just a bit spooked." He patted the mare gently, wishing he had a treat for her.

"I was actually asking about you."

"I'm fine. Really. But you look cold."

"Just a little bit."

He pulled off his scarf and dropped it around her neck before she could say no. "Maybe that will help."

"Reid…" She looked up and caught his gaze. "I have to admit it's good to be back, but nothing's changed. And nothing can change between us."

He knew she was right. He shouldn't want to kiss her, but untangling the feelings he had for her wasn't something he knew how to do. Still, her wishes were clear, and he had no plans to deviate from them.

"I understand. And I promise I'll be a perfect gentleman."

She hesitated again as she turned to watch the pinks and purples of the sunset shift above the mountains before disappearing. It was a sight he never grew tired of. This ranch was where he'd grown up. Where he'd learned to ride a horse and rope a cow. And where he'd spent hours with Claire.

But that had been another time. Another life. And maybe seeing her again and being reminded that there was no chance of their getting back together would motivate him to start looking for someone else. To stop comparing every woman he went out with to Claire.

They started back to the house by the light of the moon. He tried not to let his thoughts linger on how good it was to be with her again, and how much he'd missed her.

"I'm trying to figure out what just happened," he said. "It's like someone is trying to scare us away from investigating."

"I don't know, because it doesn't make sense. Finding a way to take either of us off the investigation wouldn't solve anything, because in the end, someone else would simply take over. It's not as if the investigation is simply going to go away and we won't find whoever is behind this."

"I agree," he said. "It doesn't make sense. I want to talk to Griffin about what just happen, but no one else for the moment."

The ranch house appeared in the distance, shrouded in darkness except for the rays of moonlight peeking out from behind the clouds. A vehicle was driving up, and he recognized his brother Liam's SUV.

"Are you ready for this?" he asked.

"I'll be fine. I always loved your family. Don't worry about me."

But that was easier said than done. He knew his brothers. They were going to make the assumption Claire had stepped back into his life, something he'd have to rectify as soon as possible.

A minute later, he was introducing Claire to Li-

FIVE

Claire's mind was still racing as Reid drove down the narrow two-lane road that led to the large O'Callaghan ranch, but there was nothing more she could do that night. They'd spent three hours going through photos while IT worked to get a higher resolution frame of their possible suspect, hoping they'd eventually be able to search for a match in the federal database.

For now, all they could do was wait and enjoy the view of Pikes Peak and the surrounding mountains. The familiar ranch, with its acres and acres of blue spruce and Douglas firs, brought with it a flood of memories. And almost made her feel as if she'd never left Timber Falls.

How many times had she gone fishing with Reid or snowmobiling on this very property and hiked in the hills to the south? They'd even ice fished one winter, then spent the rest of the evening huddled in front of the fireplace, drinking hot chocolate and laughing.

But in reality, that had been a lifetime ago. Something she couldn't forget.

Marci O'Callaghan was sitting in a padded chair on the wraparound porch with a blanket covering her as they pulled up to the two-story house.

Claire's stomach clenched at the sight of the woman who'd been nothing but kind to her.

Maybe coming had been a mistake.

"You okay?" Reid asked as he shut off the engine. He seemed to sense her mood, something he'd always been good at.

She let out a nervous laugh. "It's a little too late to turn around."

He reached out and squeezed her hand, then pulled away, as if he realized he was triggering yet another flood of memories.

She took off her seat belt, then reached for the car door handle. "I'll be fine. Just a little nervous."

"You have nothing to be nervous about. You were always my mother's favorite."

Seconds later, Marci was wrapping her arms around Claire in a huge hug. "It is so good to see you. It's been way too long."

Claire caught the older woman's gaze and smiled. "It's good to see you, as well."

And it was. Claire just wanted to forget that she'd never told the woman she had a grandson.

"I hope you don't mind my inviting you over," Marci rushed on. "I just thought it might be nice to catch up."

"It will. I'm looking forward to seeing your growing family."

"Two, soon to be three, daughters-in-law and two grandbabies." Marci laughed. "I don't think it gets much better than that."

"I'm happy for you."

"Thank you. Reid told me you're working in Denver as an arson investigator."

"I am. It's not the same as fighting fires, but I love what I do."

"I'm not surprised."

Marci turned to Reid, who was standing beside her, looking as awkward as Claire felt. "Listen, dinner's in the crockpot, and all I have to do is take a couple pies out of the oven in fifteen minutes. Why don't the two of you go for a ride and catch the sunset. The rest of the family won't be here for at least thirty minutes."

Claire glanced at Reid.

"If you're too tired…" he started.

"No, it's not that." She glanced down at the nice, black boots Tory had loaned her. "I'm not really dressed to ride."

"We've got plenty of boots and a heavier coat if you need them. What you're wearing is fine."

She hesitated again, but riding a horse wasn't what had her stomach tied up in knots. What worried her the most was Reid. She'd somehow convinced herself, when work had brought her to Timber Falls, that she wouldn't have to interact with him. That she might see him, but she definitely wouldn't spend time with him. Nothing more than a courtesy *how are you, it's been a long time*.

So how had she agreed to dinner with his entire family?

"A bit of fresh air will probably do both of you good," Marci said, interrupting her thoughts.

Claire nodded, realizing she was probably going to have regrets no matter what she did here, but at least the weather was perfect and the views stunning.

"Great." Marci waved her hand, then started toward the house. "I'll see you both back here in an hour."

am's wife, Gabby, their three-year-old, Mia, and two-month-old son, Ethan.

"Claire, it's so good to see you." Liam pulled her into a hug. "I can't believe how long it's been four... five years?"

"Almost six, actually."

"It's wonderful to meet you, and we're so glad you decided to have dinner with us," Gabby said. "It's going to be a houseful, but it should also be a lot of fun."

Claire had just shifted her attention to Mia and the baby when a second car pulled up with Griffin and Tory, and Caden and his fiancée, Gwen. Reid tried to gauge Claire's reaction to seeing everyone at once, but from the outside she seemed completely composed and relaxed, which didn't surprise him at all.

"It's good to see you again," Griffin said, stepping out of the car. "Now you can finally meet my fiancée, Tory."

"So you're the one I have to thank for the clothes," Claire said, giving Tory a hug.

"I hope you don't mind the Christmas theme," Tory said as a blush swept across her face. "I thought it might cheer you up."

"I love it," Claire said, holding open the jacket, so everyone could see the Christmas tree T-shirt. "Congrats on the upcoming wedding, and on your engagement, Caden and Gwen. There must be something in the air here."

"You might be right." Tory laughed. "And we're actually getting married here on the ranch."

"Wow... That's going to be beautiful."

"Do you remember the small chapel my grandfather built on the property?" Reid asked.

"Up on the ridge?"

He nodded as another memory surfaced of showing her one of his favorite views on the property.

"That will be stunning," Claire said. "I remember the stained-glass windows and the views from the front of the building."

"We heard about the fire at the B&B." Gwen tugged on the end of her ponytail. "I'm glad you're okay, but that had to have been frightening."

"It was, but thankfully, there were no injuries."

A bell started ringing from the porch.

"That's mom's signal that dinner is ready," Griffin said. "We probably should go. She made brisket, mashed potatoes, homemade yeast rolls…"

"I haven't forgotten what a great cook your mother is," Claire said.

"Don't worry about the horses," Caden said, pulling out his cell. "You can leave them where you have them tied, and I'll call Bruce and have him get them settled back into the barn."

Reid touched Claire's arm and caught her attention before she turned toward the house. "I'm going to talk to Griffin now, okay?"

She nodded. "Of course. I'll be fine."

Reid pulled Griffin aside and waited until the group was out of earshot, thankful Claire didn't seem to mind him leaving her on her own for a few minutes. But they both knew they couldn't ignore what just happened.

"What's going on?" Griffin asked. "Or can I assume this has something to do with Claire?"

Reid frowned. "For one, she's already made it clear that she's not interested in reliving the past and re-kindling anything that might have been between us.

Not that I was looking to do that, but two, I'm under orders to keep her safe. Nothing more."

"I'm sorry to hear that." Griffin shoved his hands into his front pockets. "I was always convinced she was the one for you."

"So was I, at one point, anyway, but I was wrong. This has nothing to do with Claire."

"Okay."

"It's possible that someone jammed her door shut the night of the fire, though we're not sure how or why. There's also evidence that points to the fact that the Rocky Mountain Arsonist was involved in the fire."

"Captain Ryder mentioned that possibility."

"And that's not all. The two of us went riding a few minutes ago, as you know, and there was a drone out there—a flame-throwing drone. It spooked my horse and I was thrown."

"What? You've got to be kidding me."

"I wish I was. I'm not sure what's going on at this point, but this has to be tied to the investigation some-how."

"I guess it's possible, but tracing a drone…that won't be easy."

"I know. But I'm worried. I might not have feelings for Claire anymore, but I still don't want anything to happen to her." Reid blew out a sharp breath of air. "And someone seems willing to do anything to stop this investigation."

SIX

Laughter erupted around the dining table of the O'Callaghan ranch house, as Caden told the story Claire had heard more than once about a rubber snake left in Griffin's boot back when the four brothers were boys. The sense of familiarity she felt sitting at the table surprised her. It was as if Reid had never left her. But that wasn't true. She was a different person than when he'd broken up with her all those years ago. Thinking she could step into Reid's family without it digging up a bucketful of memories had been a mistake.

Gwen, Caden's fiancée, scooted back from the table a couple of inches, laughing so hard tears were falling down her cheeks. "I never get tired of these stories, though I have to say, boys, your mom and dad deserve medals for raising you."

"We could go on all night," Liam said, while patting Ethan on the shoulder. "Remember the caramel-covered onions?"

"What about that mustache we drew on you, Reid?" Griffin said.

Reid rolled his eyes. "With permanent marker, no less."

"My favorites were the mashed potato and black

bean cookies Reid concocted," Caden said, "and locking Liam in the bathroom using pennies."

Pennies to lock a door?

Claire glanced at Reid. Had she mentioned the penny she found outside her room?

Liam tried to frown, but there was still a gleam in his eye as the conversation continued. "That one wasn't funny."

"Oh, it was funny," Griffin said. "What about substituting horseradish for whipped cream?"

"Wait a minute." Gabby grabbed another roll, then turned to Marci. "I want to know how you survived their childhood."

"It wasn't easy. You think your little ones are sweet at this age, but just wait. The day will come when you will have to question your sanity. Of course Reid was the most laid back of the four of them. Always content to just hang out."

"Don't try to paint him as innocent," Griffin chuckled.

"I'm curious about the pennies..." Claire set down her fork, trying to keep the fear out of her voice. "How do you lock someone in a bathroom with pennies?"

"It doesn't work with every door," Griffin said, "but it is possible—we've proved it. You jam pennies between the door and the hinge, which in turn prevents the door from opening from the inside."

Claire caught Reid's gaze for a moment, before looking away. She slid her hand into her pocket and fingered the penny she'd found on the floor outside her room. She'd tried to convince herself that all of this—the fire and the door jamming—were nothing but coincidences. That she wasn't a target, because that didn't make sense.

She didn't want that to make sense. But the drone that had attacked them tonight had changed everything.

Marci stood and started gathering plates. "I have a feeling that the four of you could go on with these stories all night, but how about some dessert? I made apple pie."

"I can help." Claire jumped to her feet and started picking up dishes. She needed a distraction, something to stop her mind from heading in the direction it was going. That someone was after her. That someone might even want her dead.

"You need to sit down and enjoy yourself," Tory said. "You've had a rough twenty-four hours, and from what I've heard, you're supposed to be resting."

Claire forced a smile. "I don't mind. I feel fine."

Ignoring the concern, she grabbed a few more plates before escaping to the kitchen, while trying to keep her panic from escalating.

"I really do wish you'd rest." Marci followed her into the kitchen with another handful of dishes. "Reid told me what happened at the bed-and-breakfast. That had to be terrifying."

"Your son saved me."

"Something like that can happen in an instant and before you know it, everything's gone. I need to go see Mike and Sarah. I heard they're staying with her sister for now. I'm guessing it's going to take quite a bit of reconstruction."

"It will, but at least no one was hurt. It could have been so much worse. And while there was a lot of damage to the downstairs, hopefully they'll be able to re-open before too long."

Marci took some small plates from a cupboard and

set them down on the counter before turning to her. "I'm grateful, as well, but I do feel like I owe you an apology. My invitation to you for dinner was purely selfish. I always enjoyed being around you and was excited to hear you were back in town, but if I overstepped my bounds and put you in an uncomfortable situation—"

"No. It's fine. I wanted to come because no matter what happened between Reid and me, I love your family and have so many great memories of this place. And while I'll admit things are a bit awkward between the two of us—at least, they were at first—our romance was a long time ago. I think we've both made peace and moved on. It was good for me to come."

"I'm glad you did."

Claire glanced at the decorated Christmas wreath hanging on the window and breathed in the smells of apple pie and cinnamon. She remembered how much Marci loved holidays and decorated for every season. And how much she'd loved being a part of their holidays when she and Reid were together.

She headed back into the dining room for another stack of dishes from the table, guilt looming inside her. While it was good to see Reid's family, the truth was that this wasn't her family and it never would be. Her mother was right. Telling the truth about Owen was only going to hurt everyone. And even if she'd been wrong about Reid's reaction, after all this time, he was never going to be able to forgive her for betraying him. No… for everyone's sake—especially Owen's—it was better to keep the past in the past and move on.

Gabby came into the kitchen behind her, carrying Ethan.

"He's such a sweet baby," Claire said, stacking up the dirty dishes.

"Thank you. I'm doing everything I can to soak up every stage, but time seems to be flying by so quickly."

"I heard you're moving to Texas," Claire said.

"Please don't remind me." Marci put her arm around Gabby's shoulders. "I'm going to have to start making frequent trips down there."

"That has to be a lot of changes for you, Gabby," Claire said.

"And for the grandma too." Marci started slicing the pie. "I was hoping I could keep all my grandkids close by, but I guess that's not realistic the way people move these days."

"It's definitely not realistic when it comes to the army," Gabby said. "But we'll be back often. I promise."

Tory stepped into the kitchen, carrying the rest of the dishes and laughing about another story that had just been told. This was what Claire had always wanted. A big family with lots of cousins and laughter getting together for holidays and enjoying shared memories.

But right now the noise was pressing in around her. Too many voices. Too many questions over past decisions, and a new fear that someone was after her. She needed to leave, but if she did that, everyone would worry about her. The bottom line was that she never should have come here. She would go to Reid and tell him she had a headache and needed to go check into a room at the hotel she planned to stay in tonight.

She forced a smile as Marci handed her a bucket of ice cream and a scoop. She couldn't tell him she had a headache. Then he'd start worrying that she was having symptoms from the fire and he'd insist on getting her checked out again at the hospital. Which really meant that she was stuck here until he was ready to head back to town.

She plopped some ice cream on a piece of pie. She could do it. Force a smile and pretend everything was okay. Pretend that it wasn't true that someone potentially wanted her dead.

"Claire?"

A hand squeezed her shoulder and she jumped. Reid stood behind her.

"Sorry… Is everything okay?"

"Yeah… I'm fine. Sorry. I've been assigned to the ice cream scoop."

"Are you having any of the symptoms the doctor told you to watch out for?"

"No, though… I guess I am a little overwhelmed and a bit tired."

"I promise not to keep you out too long, but you don't mind staying for dessert, do you?"

"Of course not. I remember how much you love anything sweet."

"It's the way to a man's heart. In the meantime, Mom wants me to go get some more logs for the fire. Why don't you come outside and get some fresh air for a moment?"

She hesitated, then nodded. Maybe that was exactly what she needed. Some fresh air would help clear her mind. And she could tell him about the penny.

She followed him outside, grateful for the quiet. The last time she'd had a panic attack had been years ago. When Owen was six months old, he'd come down with a serious respiratory virus that had kept her up for nights and escalated her anxiety. Eventually, he'd gotten over it, and she'd learned to worry less, but today had brought it all up again. One of the reasons she'd quit fighting fires was because she wanted a job that was less risky. She didn't want to ever leave Owen in a situation where his mother didn't come home. And now those fears were back.

"It's starting to snow," Reid said. "You can sit and enjoy a bit of winter in the moonlight while I gather wood. As I recall, this always was your favorite season."

"It's beautiful here no matter what season, though I think this is definitely my favorite. Snow on the mountains, skiing, Christmas lights, hot chocolate in front of the fire."

"Mine too, though watch out, I wouldn't be surprised if my mom talks us all into singing Christmas carols before the night is over."

"I wouldn't mind."

"Claire…what happened in there? It was like you froze. I was afraid having all the family here might be overwhelming. If you'd rather go back into town, we can check you into the hotel and you can get a good night's sleep. You don't have to feel bad at all. Everyone knows how much you've been through."

"I'm okay. Some fresh air is exactly what I needed."

She was avoiding telling him something. Something in there had upset her.

He started filling up the wheelbarrow with wood from the pile he'd helped chop over the summer and fall. Memories of the two of them refused to stay buried no matter how hard he tried. Some of his favorites were when they'd bundled up and gone out on the snowmobile, or settled in front of the fire drinking hot chocolate and watching movies. He'd made a mistake pushing her out of his life, but it was too late to change the past.

"I saw the look on your face when Caden was telling the story about the pennies and the locked door," he said.

"Does that really work?" she asked.

He paused in front of her. "With certain doors, yes."

"The door at the B&B?"

"Yes, actually, I think so, but what are you thinking? That someone jammed your door shut with pennies?"

She stood and pulled something out of her pocket, then handed it to him. "This was not an accident. Just like someone trying to run us off the road. Like the drone that attacked you... I don't know what's going on, but I found this outside the doorway on the floor, under the edge of the carpet."

Reid stared at the penny and felt an eerie sensation spread through him.

"I think someone used pennies to jam the door to make sure I couldn't get out of the room, then returned and took the evidence and accidently left one behind."

"I agree none of this can be a coincidence, but who? And why? We mentioned before that whoever is behind the arson fires would know that even if you were taken off the case for whatever reason, someone else would take your place. That can't be their motivation."

"I know. That's why I can't shake the feeling that this is personal somehow."

He sat down next to her, forgetting about the wood for the moment. He hadn't wanted to believe someone was trying to hurt her, but while this wasn't solid evidence, it wasn't something they could simply ignore either.

"Have you received any threats before coming here?" he asked. "Or maybe it's possible someone has a grudge against you and might want to get back at you for something."

"No. I mean, it's possible because I've had people put behind bars for starting fires, but in reality I only gather the evidence and make my conclusions. I'm not the one who prosecutes and decides what happens to the person. And I'm not sure I'm the only one they're after. We were both in the car, and that drone went after you."

"I'm going to talk to Griffin again—"

"I know we have to tell the authorities, but I don't want to be taken off the case." She rested her hand on his arm for a moment, then pulled it away. "I've been tracking down this arsonist for six months and I will find him. They already have the sheriff's department on alert and you watching over my shoulder."

Flakes of snow lay scattered across her hair and the moonlight lit her up from behind. He wished he could forget everything that had happened between them, that he could convince himself he'd moved on and that seeing her standing in front of him didn't affect him.

Except it did.

And now he was worried someone wanted to hurt her…

"If someone did lock you in that room and then set the house on fire, we're talking about attempted murder, Claire. And if it is the arsonist behind the fire, then you know more than anyone what he is capable of doing. He's responsible for millions of dollars of damages, but on top of that two men are dead because of those fires."

"I know."

"I want you to stay here at my parents' place while

you're in town, but don't tell anyone where you are. I'll stay here, as well. Caden has a house just down the road, and Griffin will be on call."

"You don't think that's taking things a bit over the top?"

He frowned at her stubbornness. "Not at all. It seems like a practical solution to me."

"I don't know. I've been talking to your sisters-in-law. You O'Callaghan brothers tend to like to play the hero."

"There's nothing wrong with that, especially when there's a beautiful woman in danger involved."

"Really?"

"I didn't mean…not that you aren't beautiful, because you are, but I meant—"

She shifted toward him and smiled. "I know what you meant and I'm just teasing you. But you have to admit it is a bit… I don't know…romantic."

"Romantic?"

"No?" she asked.

Reid took in a deep breath, wishing she didn't affect him the way she did. "That's just not the word I thought you were going to use."

"From what I've heard, playing hero has also been pretty personal. Gabby found evidence that her husband might have been murdered and then someone came after her and Liam saved her life. Then Griffin ended up playing bodyguard for Tory who was almost killed because she was a key witness in a crime."

"And don't forget that Caden and Gwen were mixed up in a hostage situation."

"Yep. There is definitely something about your family that seems to attract trouble."

"Or maybe we're just good at getting people out of trouble."

Reid resisted the urge to pull her against him. His brothers might have found happily ever after, but he wasn't going to this time. Not with Claire. Even if he tried to play the hero. And that was something he couldn't forget.

SEVEN

At nine the next morning, Claire was sitting in the passenger seat of Reid's pickup truck while he drove her to the scene of the fire she'd originally come to investigate. Thirty-six hours ago, she never would have imagined Reid O'Callaghan playing the role of her personal bodyguard. But he was. On top of that, while yesterday's dinner with his entire family had left her feeling vulnerable, even that didn't compare to the fact that someone seemed determined to hurt her and Reid. Which was why she'd agreed to stay at the ranch until they were able to dig up the truth.

"I was afraid my bodyguard might have overslept," Claire said, grasping the travel mug of coffee his mother had handed her as they headed out the door.

"Hardly," he said. "How late did you stay up?"

"Not late, though I was awake before the sun." She studied the scenery on either side of the narrow dirt road they were headed down, with its patches of snow on the ground and mountain views in the background. "I don't remember ever coming out to this farm."

"Hazel and Bill Reynolds have lived here...I don't know...as long as I can remember. They have two sons who have both moved to Texas. One of them was able to return after the fire and help out some, but last I heard they were thinking about moving to be closer to their boys."

"That has to be a tough decision."

"I'm sure it is. While living near their boys would be a blessing for them, leaving everything they know can't be easy." Reid made another turn down a long driveway, then parked his truck near the charred structure on the east side of the property. "I called and told them we were going to come and look at the damage to their barn and equipment. They're at the doctor right now, but said that would be fine."

"Is one of them sick?" Claire asked.

"I know she's been struggling with anxiety since the fire, but I don't have any details."

"I'm sorry to hear that, though I would like to talk to them. They have to be grateful their house wasn't damaged."

"Definitely, and they said they would be back as soon as they could. Captain Ryder should be here any minute too. I think he just wants to touch base with you."

Claire stepped out of the truck with the case file in hand and started around the perimeter of the charred building. While she'd already looked at photos of the evidence from the fire, seeing the scene for herself was essential.

Reid kept a few steps behind her as she slowly made her way around the outside. Grass had started growing back in a few places, but for the most part, nothing had changed from the photos in the file she'd been given.

"If you don't mind me asking," Reid said, "why an arson investigator?"

She mulled over the question while continuing to take in the scene and debated how to answer it without bringing up their son. "I loved working as a firefighter, but the whole investigation behind the fire has always fascinated me. And I guess when you consider that arson accounts for billions of dollars of lost or damaged property every year and only a small percentage of the arsonists are actually arrested, I like the fact that I'm helping people who are impacted."

"It almost sounds…personal."

"I have a friend back in Denver whose house burned down and it was suspected as being an arson fire. Thankfully, she and her family were okay, but they never caught who started the fire. More than likely it was a couple kids in the neighborhood, but we'll probably never know. And while the majority of fires are set in order to try and scam insurance policies, I was struck by how, in a short instant, the devastation it leaves behind can change everything."

"That is true."

"And the complexity of most investigations makes it a challenge. Unfortunately, with the majority of arson cases the perpetrator is never caught."

"You always did love a challenge," he said.

"Funny." She stopped and caught his gaze, wishing those blue eyes of his didn't seem just as mesmerizing as they had all those years ago. She cleared her throat. "Think about it. You're looking at a crime where most of the evidence can be destroyed, either from the fire or from the foam used to put out the fire. So in the end, we have to rely on people like you, the firefighters, along with anyone else who might have witnessed something."

"True."

Claire pulled out the photos from the investigation she'd printed out. "Can you walk me through the fire?"

"Of course. It started in the northwest corner of the barn."

She followed him to the spot that had been marked on one of her photos. "An accelerant was found here."

"Yes," he said. "Traces of acetone and gasoline were found."

"And the antique lighter? Where was it discovered?"

Reid walked another six feet to the left. "Here."

She held up the photo. The fire had spread quickly, destroying the integrity of the structure, as well as the majority of the equipment, before it was put out. Thankfully, according to her notes, there had been little wind that night, so the flames didn't spread to the main house or any other outlying buildings.

"What do you know about the couple?" Claire asked, continuing to walk around the damaged structure.

"Are you asking if they might have started the fire themselves for an insurance payoff?"

Her jaw tensed at the question. "You know I have to look at that. There was no evidence of a forced entry, for starters."

"I just can't imagine they were involved. They go to our church, and I've known them for years."

"Going to church doesn't make someone innocent."

"That's true."

She caught his gaze and studied his expression, trying to figure out what was niggling at her. "You surprise me."

"Because I go to church?"

"It's not just that. There's just something… I don't know…something different about you."

She couldn't put a finger on what it was. He was still just as good-looking and charming as the first day they'd met, but it wasn't his appearance she was referring to.

"I've changed a lot since you saw me last," he said.

"I guess you're not the only person who's changed."

While she'd gone to church with Reid's family occasionally while they'd dated, she'd never had a faith of her own until after Owen was born. Back then she'd been focused on her career and her relationship with Reid, not trying to understand what it meant to serve God.

Reid stepped in front of her. "What are you thinking?"

She turned away from him, not ready to share her real thoughts. "I was thinking that the actual fire definitely fits the pattern. There's both the combination of accelerants that was found at other fires as well as the antique lighter."

"But…"

She shook her head. "So far the arsonist has never struck more than one time in any town."

"So twice in one town doesn't fit the profile."

"Not so far, but it might be insignificant. The MOs and patterns can change. That's typical. And the antique lighters. That's the key as far as I'm concerned. We've managed to keep that detail out of the news so far."

"We've looked at photos from the scene. What about comments left on news sites or social media? Have you looked at those?"

"Yes, and so far there hasn't been any obvious person who stands out."

The sound of vehicles pulled her attention to the

driveway and away from the charred remains. Captain Ryder arrived right behind the Reynoldses. Reid quickly made introductions as soon as they'd stepped out of the vehicles.

"Mr. and Mrs. Reynolds, it's nice to meet you, though I'm so sorry for the loss of your property. I know the fire did a lot of damage and the cleanup and dealing with insurance can't be easy."

"Please…it's Bill and Hazel," Bill said, "and thank you. You're right, it has been hard. We lost most of our winter food supply, so in a way we feel like we're starting over again."

Claire clutched the folder under her arm. "I know you've already talked to the authorities. I'm just following up on a few questions so we can officially close the case."

Bill glanced at his wife. "We were told this could have been started by an arsonist."

"Unfortunately, we don't have an answer for that right now," Captain Ryder said. "Which is why we asked for help from Denver."

Claire chose her words carefully. "What I can tell you is that there were several things in the final report that were flagged. I'm here to sign off on them. It's all a part of the process."

"Like we told Reid, you're welcome to look around," Bill said. "We're ready for the investigation to be over so we can start cleaning up."

"Reid said he'd heard you might be selling the property?" Claire asked.

"We're not sure we have a choice. Insurance will give us a payout…eventually…but in the meantime we're struggling to keep things up. And it's looking like even with a payout it's not going to cover replacement costs for everything that was lost." Bill laid his hand on his wife's arm and frowned. "We've lived here our entire lives, but I have to say, in the back of our minds we've been looking at moving closer to our kids anyway. And while they love coming up here and visiting, maybe it's time."

"I know that decision can't be easy," Captain Ryder said.

"Starting over at our age seems like climbing a mountain."

"I understand," Claire said. "Is there anything else that you think I should know? Anything odd that might have happened since the fire that you haven't told anyone about?"

"No." Bill shook his head, then looked to his wife. "I don't think so. Other than the stress. The whole situation has been unsettling."

"Wait. There is one thing," Hazel said. "It's probably not important, but on the day of the fire, we did realize we couldn't find the key to the barn."

"She's right." Bill's phone rang and he pulled it out of his pocket. "I'm sorry, but I need to take this."

"No problem." Claire glanced at her notebook as the man stepped away. "You couldn't find the key?"

"That's right."

"We were told there was no sign of forced entry," Claire said. "That could explain how someone got in. Where did you normally keep the keys?"

"On a hook in the house, near the back door. Which probably wasn't the smartest thing because we only keep things locked up at night, but we never worried about things like that."

"So someone could have slipped in and taken the key," Claire said.

"If they knew where to look, I suppose. Yes."

Claire reached into her jacket pocket and pulled out a business card. "I need to spend a few more minutes looking around, but if you or your husband think of anything else, feel free to give me a call."

"And I have a few more questions I need to ask you both," Captain Ryder said.

"Of course," Hazel said. "We need this investigation finished so we can tear down the structure."

Bill walked back to them, a frown on his face.

"Is everything okay?" Reid asked.

"We forgot one of Hazel's prescriptions at the pharmacy."

"Listen," Reid said, "I'll head back into town and pick it up while Claire and Captain Ryder finish here."

"You don't have to do that."

"It's not a problem at all," Reid said.

"If you're sure," Bill said. "Thank you. And we're happy to answer any questions you have."

"I need to grab another camera battery out of your vehicle," Claire said to Reid.

Reid turned to her as they walked back to the truck. "You won't need me for the next thirty minutes, will you?"

"I pretty sure the captain can handle my security."

Claire smiled ignoring the flirtatious tone of his voice. Reid always had been able to bypass any walls around her heart, and apparently nothing had changed.

"By the way," Reid said, heading for his truck, ignoring her grin that seemed to pierce right through his defenses, "when's the last time you had something to eat? My mom said you didn't eat breakfast."

"I had some coffee."

He pulled out his keys and stopped. "That's not breakfast. I'm going to bring you back something," he said. "It hasn't been so long that I've forgotten your favorites. Unless you don't like Jimmy's slow-cooked pulled pork, served on a freshly baked brioche roll with homemade BBQ sauce and a side of Jimmy's slaw anymore."

"Reid… Yes, I still love Jimmy's pulled pork, but you don't have to do that."

"I know, but I would hate for you to suddenly pass out while working a case, because I don't know if you've heard, but there can be serious side effects from going without Jimmy's pulled pork for too long."

"Seriously?"

"Oh, yeah…and for you we're not talking days or weeks, we're talking years. There is no telling what could happen."

"You're impossible."

"Maybe, but don't say I didn't warn you. I've been craving some myself and it's barely been a week." He hesitated, realizing how easy it was to flirt with her, to almost forget that they weren't together anymore.

"I suppose if you need an excuse to get it for yourself, you could bring me some and I won't turn it down."

"I think I will."

"And Reid…"

He headed toward his truck, but her voice stopped him.

"Thanks for offering to go into town. They seem like such a sweet couple. I feel sorry for them."

"It's not a problem."

She took a step toward him. "Does Jimmy's still have those banana chocolate shakes?"

"With added M&Ms?"

She nodded.

"I suppose I could manage that, though I don't want you to get spoiled having a bodyguard/chauffeur catering to your every whim. You know that this is only until we catch whoever's behind these fires."

"Don't worry. I don't plan to take advantage of you."

Reid jumped into the truck, his eyes still on her as she headed back to the barn. He shouldn't be flirting with her. He knew better than that. It was only going to get him into trouble, or at the least lead him to another broken heart. Why was it so easy to slip into those old habits? She'd always made him laugh. That was something that had drawn him to her at the beginning. She was the ultimate optimist and saw good in everything and everyone.

The last few years, though, seemed to have mellowed her. Maybe it was her job that had sobered her. Maybe it was simply a part of growing up. They'd both grown up, changed, and what he used to know about her didn't necessarily hold true for where either of them were today. That was something he couldn't forget.

He pulled out an old strip of photos of them he kept on the back of the visor. They'd gone ice skating that night, then taken a walk through town to see the Christmas lights. Eventually he'd pulled her into the photo booth where they'd taken a string of silly photos. In the last one, he'd pulled her against him and kissed her, capturing both the surprise in her eyes and the smile on her lips.

He shoved the photos back. He should have thrown them away years ago, because they represented everything he wanted to forget.

He tapped the brake as he took another turn on the curvy road. He'd eventually decided that the only way to move on with his life was to find someone else who could make him happy, someone who could make him forget. So he'd started dating again, but no matter how many women he went out with, it never covered up the pain of his mistakes with Claire. It was why he'd told her he couldn't imagine having a family of his own. It wasn't that he didn't want one, but no one he'd known had ever managed to compare to Claire.

The white truck appeared out of nowhere behind him. Reid sped up, then pulled over to let it pass. Instead, it got closer to his bumper. A second later, it rammed into him from behind. Reid felt the sharp jolt from the impact as he fought to keep his truck from flipping as he went around another curve.

The list of facts from the investigation surfaced. Claire being locked in her room during the fire. The drone in the woods… Nothing made sense. Why would someone come after him?

The white truck slammed into him again. He fumbled for his phone while trying to keep his vehicle on the road. He needed to call 911. But it was too late. His truck flipped twice, landed upside down, then skidded across the narrow road before slamming into a tree.

EIGHT

This fire definitely hadn't been an accident.

Claire looked through her notes on her tablet while the captain spoke with the Reynoldses and she waited on a chair on their front porch for Reid to return. There were simply too many signs of arson, including the antique lighter that had been left behind. The damage was extensive with multiple points of origin. The presence of accelerants was also significant, along with the missing key the owners had just reported.

But she couldn't completely dismiss the possibility that the Reynoldses had started the fire in order to cash in their insurance policy. It happened far too often to ignore. But while it might be possible, it didn't seem a real probability, especially since they had no way to know about the antique lighters. As far as she was concerned, everything pointed to this fire being connected with the Rocky Mountain Arsonist.

The problem was, they still had no firm leads on who that was, which was frustrating. People committed arson for a number of reasons and figuring out the motive could help investigators track down who was behind them. But in this case, the clues all stopped just short of giving them those answers. While some did it simply to vandalize, situations like this all pointed to something far more complex and planned out. It might be someone seeking thrills or attention, or satisfying some hero complex. It also could be tied into someone suffering from pyromania. But whatever it was, they needed to find the person.

They'd checked crime scene photos of the crowds to see if there was someone who'd showed up at the different fires. Their only possible suspect was the man wearing the hoodie, but without a clearer photo, they'd been unable to ID him.

Which left her going back to the one common denominator: the antique lighter.

It was a definite clue, but so far they hadn't been able to trace where they'd come from. The work was slow and tedious and, at the moment, frustrating, but sometimes all it took was one small detail that would throw the case open and allow them to solve it.

A call came in on her phone as she started making a to-do list. "Mom…hey… Is everything okay?"

"Everything is fine here. You're the one I was worried about actually. I just wanted to check in on you. How are you feeling? Any symptoms related to the smoke inhalation?"

Claire set her iPad on the chair and moved to lean against the railing. "I'm fine, Mom. I promise."

"How did you sleep?"

"Pretty well. I suppose I have a lot on my mind, but that's to be expected."

"Of course it is. That fire had to be frightening, no matter how experienced you are."

Claire's fingers gripped the wooden railing and she

tried to ignore the tug on her heart. "How's Owen? I miss him."

"He misses you too, but he's fine. I'm keeping him busy."

"I appreciate it. I don't like being away from him."

"He's content to just hang out with me. We've already cleaned up the yard, made chocolate cookies and finished two puzzles."

Content just to hang out. Just like his father used to be.

Claire pushed back the thought.

"I meant to ask you where you were staying now," her mom said.

"I…" She hesitated. She wasn't going to mention the fact she was staying at the O'Callaghan ranch. "I found another place just outside of town. It's comfortable and will be fine for a few more days."

"So you're not sure when you're coming back?" her mom asked.

"These investigations have to be thorough, and there've been a couple complications. But if you need me to come back because of Owen—"

"No, of course not. He's not a problem at all. He did struggle to fall asleep last night, but we found his missing favorite pillow, prayed for you, and he was fine."

"I'll be home as soon as I can. I promise."

"Please don't worry. We both miss you, but we're fine."

"Listen, I need to go, but call me when Owen gets back from school and I'll try to pick up."

"Sounds good. Oh, and Claire…before you hang up, you haven't mentioned Reid. Have you seen him?"

Claire let out a sharp huff of air. "I have, actually, but everything's fine between us."

"You did the right thing back then," her mom said. "I know you haven't always felt like it, but trust me, he didn't want a family, and telling him would have pushed him away further and made him resent you. Now it's better just to leave things the way they are."

"Maybe." Claire reached her hand up and rubbed the back of her neck, trying to wish away the tension. "What I do know is that I'm here to do a job, not catch up with Reid. I'll be home in a couple days. I promise."

She hung up the phone, then sat back down on the padded chair. That uncomfortable gnawing feeling was back again, the one she hadn't been able to shake since she'd returned. Every time she looked at Reid, she saw Owen. And it wasn't just the facial features. They both stuck their tongue out when concentrating and neither of them liked their food touching.

But her mother was right. They might have both grown up over the past few years, but he'd made it clear that he was no closer to wanting a family than he'd been back then.

She shook off the guilt and went back to her list.

Captain Ryder stepped out of the house and onto the porch.

"Captain…" She caught the concern in his expression. "Is everything all right?"

"I got a call from the sheriff's department." He stopped in front of her, his phone still in his hand. "There's been an accident."

"What do you mean?"

"I don't have a lot of details, but Reid's truck flipped halfway between here and town."

"Reid." A wave of dizziness swept through her. "Is he okay?"

"I don't know. It sounds like someone tried to run him off the road."

Claire struggled to catch a breath. If anything happened to him...

"Claire...are you okay?"

"Yes...no. Not really."

"I understand the two of you were friends from way back?"

"We were. Back in Denver."

Serious enough I thought I'd marry him one day.

The captain motioned her toward his car. "I'll drive you to the hospital."

She slid into the passenger seat, then snapped on her seat belt. He had to be fine. They'd probably just taken him there to make sure he was okay.

"I don't mean to be nosy, but I always thought there was a broken heart in his past. Am I guessing right that it was you?"

She tried unsuccessfully to swallow the lump in her throat. "It was a long time ago. This is the first time we've seen each other in years, actually. And the weird thing is, it almost seems like no time has passed in some ways. I mean, we've both changed and grown up, but he...he's still Reid. I didn't realize how much I've missed him." She clasped her hands in her lap. "I'm sorry. I'm rambling."

"You just found out someone you care about—someone we both care about—was in an accident. You don't owe me any kind of apology. He's someone I'd trust with my life, which is why I asked him to keep an eye on you."

"I appreciate that, though…"

"What is it?"

She hesitated, trying to organize her thoughts. "We need to find out who's behind these attacks."

"Yes, we do."

"I guess Reid told you I'm convinced now that the door to my room at the B&B was jammed."

"He did."

"But now…none of this makes sense. I can't figure out the connection. These attacks…"

"Griffin has kept me in the loop with everything that's happened. I promise we'll sit down and try to figure out what's going on, but I want to get you both somewhere safe in the meantime."

Ten minutes later, they pulled up in front of the Timber Falls Clinic's emergency entrance and hurried inside.

"We're looking for Reid O'Callaghan."

"I'm sorry, we can't give out patient information."

Claire was reaching for her badge when she saw Marci hurrying across the white tile toward them. "I can."

"Please tell me he's okay."

Marci laid her hand on Claire's arm. "I'll do better than that. I'll take you to him. He's been worried about you."

"So he's…okay?"

"He is. The doctor thinks it's just a sprained wrist. He's waiting to get it x-rayed, so beyond being irritated over all of this, he'll be fine."

He was sitting on the edge of a bed in a curtained-off section, a scowl on his face.

"Reid?" She hurried to him and wrapped her arms around his neck.

"Ouch…"

"I'm sorry." She stepped back, realizing what she'd just done. "I… I was worried."

"Yeah… I'm okay. Just a sprained wrist."

"I know. I just… I just thought it might be something serious after everything that's happened."

He shot her a grin. "The accounts of my death are highly exaggerated."

"Funny."

"I'm okay. Really."

She nodded, but his assurances weren't enough. Maybe her heart shouldn't care so much, but what if the next time—if there was a next time—he ended up with something far worse than simply a sprained wrist?

Reid studied Claire's expression, unsure of how to react to her. When she'd walked into the room with the captain, her hug had thrown him off. And from the look on her face it had surprised her, as well. Of course, it wasn't the first time he'd failed to understand her.

"What happened?" the captain asked.

"I already gave a brief statement to the sheriff. All I can really know is that a truck came out of nowhere and ran into my bumper twice. The second time it ran me off the road and my truck flipped, then hit a tree."

"If all you got out of that was a sprained wrist, then we have a lot to be thankful for," Claire said, perching on the end of the bed.

"Yes, but we have another problem to deal with," the captain said. "Claire and I were talking on the way here. Clearly this, like the other incidents, was no accident.

And while I don't know what's going on, I'm pretty sure our arsonist is here in Timber Falls. And the two of you—for whatever reason—are targets."

Claire gripped the bed rail. "We need to come up with a plan. If we don't stop the attacks, this person's actions could escalate even further. And we need to figure out the connection. Why might someone be after both of us?"

The captain's phone rang, and he checked the caller ID. "Sorry, but I'm going to have to take this."

"We need to reevaluate every piece of evidence, from every one of the fires," Claire said, turning back to Reid as the captain left the room. "We'll examine the photos from the crime scene, every spectator and every mention on social media. We need to create an updated timeline so we can see if there's a pattern we're missing. The bottom line is we know he's here, in town, and we need to tighten the noose around his neck and bring him in."

She'd stood and began pacing the tiled floor, so he decided to close his mouth and just let her vent.

"What I'm struggling to understand is how the fires are connected to the attacks against us, personally. There are too many moving parts that don't make sense, but if we pull them apart and look at them side by side, we might be able to figure it out."

She took a deep breath and stopped next to him. He reached out and squeezed her hand.

"We're going to find him," Reid said.

"I know." A blush crossed her cheeks as her gaze dropped. "And I'm sorry. I didn't mean to completely lose it. I'm just... I'm feeling like things are spinning out of control and we need to find a way to put an end to this. We can't have anyone else hurt. Next time we might be looking at far more than a sprained wrist. You could have died."

Reid swallowed hard at her answer. "Is that what all of this is about? You thought I was dead?"

"With everything that has been going on, yes, I was worried about you. We might not have seen each other for a long time, but I still care. I wouldn't want anything to happen to you…"

"But I didn't die, and I'm barely hurt."

She cocked her head and shot him a smile. "Okay, the truth is, you were supposed to get me a pork sandwich and shake, and now I'm starving."

"So this is all about BBQ and the shake I promised?"

She nodded, but there was a spark in her eyes.

He couldn't figure her out. One moment she seemed to want to put as much distance between them as possible, and the next she seemed to want to bridge the wall separating them.

"Actually, I'm flattered," he said. "Now I know if something happened to me, you'd miss me at least a little bit."

"Of course I'd miss you. Jokes aside, this is serious. We can place the arsonist here a week ago, and more recently at the B&B, and then again this morning in a white pickup." Claire blew out a deep breath. "This wasn't a random case of road rage. You were targeted and we need to know why. Especially if he wants you out of the way for some reason."

"Yes, but why would he? That's what doesn't make sense. I'm not essential to this case. I'm just a firefighter who was at the scene of the crime. What are they doing? Trying to get rid of me so they can get to you? That doesn't make any sense."

But she was right about one thing. He'd seen his truck after they pulled him out of the wreck and helped him walk away. He shouldn't have come out of it with just a sprained wrist. The pickup was totaled, and while he could joke and make light of the situation, if any variables had changed, he wouldn't be here talking to her.

"Did you get a license plate number?" she asked.

She pulled out her notebook, the seriousness of her actions clear as she leaned forward. He couldn't help but smile at her familiar notebook and the pages of lists and notes she'd meticulously taken. Some things never changed.

"It was a white truck, but I didn't see the plate. The sheriff's going to check security cameras in town and see if they can track it and get a license number."

"Good. I'm just… I'm glad you're okay."

She took a few notes, then caught his gaze and hesitated as if she wanted to tell him something. Reid started to ask what was on her mind but Captain Ryder stepped back into the room.

"I've just been out talking with your brother, Griffin," the captain said. "The sheriff's department is going to open an investigation into the hit and run."

"Good," Reid said. He glanced through the partially open curtain to the busy hallway. "As soon as I get my X-ray, I'll be good to go, though the doctor is convinced it's just a sprain."

"You need to rest," Claire said.

"A little pain medicine and I'll be fine."

The captain turned to Claire. "I can have your car brought here if you'd like, but I want you both to stay at the ranch and lay low for the next few days. You'll be safe there and you can work through the evidence and see if you can come up with something you missed. But no more investigating at the scene for the moment."

Reid nodded, surprised at how the upside of all of this had turned out to be the chance to spend more time with Claire. Except he really shouldn't enjoy her being back so much. Just because some of the embers between them had never died out, didn't mean he needed to pursue her.

He would stick around, but only to make sure she stayed safe. Nothing more.

NINE

Claire stifled a yawn as they pulled into the driveway of his parents' house in her car. The sun had set hours ago, and moonlight revealed a dusting of white across the landscape that made the white Christmas lights on the house seem even more lovely. She breathed in deeply the scent of the snow and fresh air as she walked toward the house, while Reid let Sasha out of the car, trying to calm her anxiety, but it did little to help. Because the source of her current restlessness was clear.

Reid.

"It's beautiful out here, isn't it?" he said, as Sasha ran around them.

She stopped at the bottom of the porch stairs, soaking in the star-laden sky above them that she never saw in the city. But even the starlight couldn't compete with the man standing next to her. They'd been working too close for too long. Having him in the room with her at the sheriff's office while they combed through every piece of evidence they'd collected had kept her distracted. She could smell the familiar scent of his aftershave and see the warmth in his eyes when she managed to sneak a peek at him.

It wasn't the first time she'd wrestled with telling him the truth about Owen. All her excuses seemed empty and insignificant, except one thing that continued to stop her. He'd broken up with her six years ago because she was ready for marriage and a family and he wasn't. And apparently nothing had changed in all these years.

Reid, there's something you need to know about me... about us... We have a son. I have a million and one excuses, but I'm truly sorry I never told you.

No, the reality was that it was better if he never knew the truth. She wasn't prepared to deal with his reaction or with how his knowing would change everything. He had his own life to live, and saddling him with an instant family wasn't fair. And neither would she do anything to jeopardize Owen's well-being.

"It's been a long day and I'm sure you're tired," he said, starting up the stairs ahead of her.

"I am, but it's so beautiful out here with the snow and the Christmas lights from the house."

"My mother loves the holidays and uses every excuse to decorate."

"I don't blame her."

He stopped at the top of the stairs. "Are you okay? I know there's a lot going on, but you seem...I don't know...distracted."

"There's just a lot on my mind." She glanced at the porch swing. "I think I'm going to sit out here a few minutes. Try and clear my mind so it's not running all night. Though I'm not sure that's possible."

"Need some company? Unless you want to be alone—"

"I don't mind." She sat down, wondering why she'd

agreed to let him join her. Her plan had been to forget Reid and their past, not let him in. "How's your wrist?"

"Just a dull pain. The brace seems to be helping some."

"That's good. I keep thinking how much worse it could have been."

"I'll admit, I do too."

"You don't get these kinds of views in the city," she said, pulling her scarf closer around her neck while staring out across the shadowy landscape.

"Have you ever thought about moving out of the city?" he asked.

"Not really. I don't think a department in a small town like Timber Falls would be able to hire a full-time arson inspector, and I love what I do. And besides that, my mother's getting older, and I think it's important I'm near her."

"I understand." The chain of the porch swing creaked as he rocked back and forth, competing with a coyote howling in the distance. "Nights like this keep me here. And I love having my family nearby. I just can't imagine living anywhere else again."

"When I'm here, I can understand that. I don't think I'll ever tire of the views, or the fresh air."

Owen would love this.

The thought took her off guard. She pressed her lips together, wishing she had the courage to simply spout out what she was thinking.

"Everything has been so focused on the fires, I'd love to hear what you've been doing the past five years."

His question shifted her train of thought. This was what she'd been wanting to avoid—anything personal between them. Something she'd managed—at least for the most part—so far. Having him around her was doing things to her heart she didn't want to admit even to herself. She'd closed off her heart to Reid O'Callaghan years ago.

At least she'd thought she had.

"I'm not sure there's a lot to say. It's hard to believe we've been apart almost six years." She struggled with what to say. "I had thought for a long time about making the switch from a firefighter to an arson inspector. So I ended up doing the needed additional training for the job, applied and got the position."

"I'm proud of you. The job seems to fit you."

"I've learned a lot and continue to learn, but I love the entire process of finding the source of a fire. The downside is that too many arsonists end up not getting caught."

"Then they better watch out now that you're on the job."

She laughed, but her smile only served to cover up her real feelings. Her mother had convinced her that she'd done the right thing six years ago, but looking at Reid now, she was beginning to wonder if she'd been wrong. Keeping the truth—and his son—from him wasn't fair. But she also knew that everything would change once she told him. That was what had always terrified her. She'd seen the consequences. But had fear blinded her? Reid was nothing like her father. And even if he didn't want a family, should she assume that he was going to react the way her father had?

On top of that, there were other issues she was going to face soon, as well. Owen was five, old enough to start asking questions about where his father was. And if she did tell Reid the truth, she was going to have to deal with having him back in their lives if that was what he decided he wanted. It was going to affect his family and any possible relationship he was involved in. And that scared her, maybe even more than losing him had. She didn't want their son to be affected by decisions she'd made in the past. She'd just been so set on moving forward after she'd found out she was pregnant.

Why is this so hard, God?

Had she really thought she'd never have to deal with this again? Never have to deal with Reid?

"Still lost in thought?"

She cleared her throat, still grabbing for answers. For someone who liked to work everything out in to-do lists and spreadsheets, this was proving to be harder than she'd ever imagined.

"Just wondering about the same question you asked me," she said finally. "What have you been doing since I last saw you?"

"I too love my job. I started a fire prevention training program at the local schools and take Sasha with me sometimes."

"I bet the students love her."

"It's fun and the kids seem to react well to her."

"She's sweet," Claire said. "And I guess we've both grown a lot over the past few years."

"I would hope so. I've gotten involved at church, as well."

She felt herself slowly relaxing as they talked, and was reminded again just how much she'd always enjoyed being with him. "I'm in a small group that has changed my perspective. The people there have made me realize that what I needed was faith."

"I know exactly what you mean." Reid's phone rang and he pulled it out of his pocket. "Hang on, it's Griffin. Maybe he's got something for us."

Reid put the call on speaker. "What's up?"

"I'm headed home now, but we just got a hit on the license plate of that truck."

"That's great," Reid said.

"We didn't find the actual truck, but it belongs to a couple here in town. Unfortunately, that doesn't help us because the truck was stolen. Elton and his wife flew out of Denver a week ago for Florida with their kids and won't be back for another three days."

"So a dead end," Reid said.

"It's looking that way. I'm heading out to their place on my way home to see if we can come up with some fingerprints there, but I'm not hopeful. We'll keep looking for the truck and hope we can pull some prints that way."

"If you need us at all—"

"I have orders that the two of you are supposed to be laying low right now. And besides, I have a feeling you could both use some sleep. I'll give you an update if I find anything out."

Reid hung up and leaned his head back, irritated, she was sure, that they were facing yet another dead end.

"That's disappointing," she said.

"It is. Though if we can find the truck, there's a good chance we can get fingerprints and figure out who was driving it. But in the meantime, we're going to have to keep looking at other avenues."

She tried to ignore the frustration that kept rearing

its ugly head, but couldn't shake the feeling that no matter what she decided, someone was going to get hurt.

Reid shared her disappointment, but the case they were working on wasn't the only thing plaguing him. He'd always wondered what might have happened if he hadn't panicked when she first brought up marriage. What would have happened if he'd simply told her he needed time? Instead, he'd lost her.

"I admit, I imagined you would have found someone and settled down now that you're pushing thirty," he said, not sure why he felt the need to broach the subject.

"Life is busy, and I'd rather wait and find the right person." He heard a soft sigh escape her lips. "So you're not dating anyone either?"

"Never anything serious. And I have Sasha to keep me company. I'm living just up the mountain in the Fox house."

"Wait a minute…you live in their cabin?"

"I do."

"I remember how incredible that view is. I'd love to see it again. The view, I mean."

"It is. And I'd love to take you there. Unfortunately, it's a temporary arrangement. They're down in Florida and asked me to housesit. My lease was expiring, and I said why not? The location's perfect. It actually isn't far from town, but you feel like you're on the edge of the world. I moved in over a year ago, and they decided not to come back for the summer and stayed with their kids. So I'm there at least until they decide to return."

"I have to say, I might be a bit jealous. I bought a house a year ago and while I love it, it still has the feel of the city and definitely no view."

He studied her face in the glow of the string of lights hanging over them, surprised someone hadn't snatched her up years ago. And relieved.

The thought threw him off. The truth was that it didn't matter if she was married or engaged. He'd blown it with her, and in a couple of days, she'd be out of his life again and he wouldn't have to worry about the woman who'd once stolen his heart. That was all in the past.

But if that was true, then why was his heart racing just sitting next to her?

"I'll be honest. I missed you," he said. "I tried to call you after I broke up with you."

"I know, I just… I was hurt and afraid."

"I never should have walked away."

He reached forward automatically and brushed an imaginary piece of lint off her shoulder. He'd forgotten how beautiful she was. But his heart hadn't forgotten. The magnetic pull he'd always felt toward her tugged at him, and suddenly, all he wanted to do was kiss her and prove that his heart hadn't forgotten.

He leaned forward, unable to resist the impulse.

"I really want to kiss you right now," he said, hesitating.

Her eyes widened, but she didn't move away. "And I think I'd really like you to kiss me right now."

The front door to the house opened as he brushed his lips across hers.

He turned around. "Mom?"

His mother stepped out onto the porch, stopping momentarily to straighten the wreath hanging on the door. "Sorry, you two. I didn't know anyone was out here. I was just going to grab my book and turn off the Christmas lights."

"That's fine." Claire stood. "I need to go to bed. It's been a long day, and I'm starting to feel it."

"Any progress on the case?" his mom asked, picking up the book.

"Nothing significant, but we're still working on it."

"I'm going to assume you ate dinner hours ago, but if you're hungry, there's a fresh batch of chocolate chip cookies on the kitchen counter."

"Thanks Mom. I appreciate it."

"I'll let you turn off the lights."

"Of course. Good night."

"Good night."

"I really should go to bed," Claire said. "I need to be able to function tomorrow and it's already past eleven."

An awkward vibe settled in between them.

"Claire…about what just happened."

"Forget it," she said. "We've both been under a lot of strain and now being back together just adds to it. It's normal that some of the old feelings we had would surface. But this…you and me… I was wrong. I can't go there again. We can't go there. This was a mistake."

"I'm sorry."

"It's not your fault. You and I have a tendency to act before we think, but I'm not that person anymore, and I don't think you are either."

He nodded, but he didn't want a clinical explanation of what he was feeling. Despite everything she was saying, he wanted to kiss her again and prove to her that she was feeling the same thing he was.

But he also knew deep down that she was right. His

emotions were pulling him to a place he didn't want to go. A place that they both would only regret.

"Good night, Reid."

"Good night."

He watched as she went into the house, shutting the door behind her. He wished he knew how to do the same thing with his heart. To close it off from her and those simmering feelings that had never completely died out. Funny how he'd thought he'd finally gotten over her after all these years and now, seeing her again, it almost seemed like she'd never left.

Reid hurried down the stairs of the front porch and along the driveway toward the barn. He needed to clear Claire out of his mind. A car motor caught his attention. The hairs on his neck prickled. They'd decided he and Claire would be safe here. He was planning to stay for a couple of days; his parents were here and Caden and a handful of ranch hands lived on the property. Everyone had been told to keep an eye out for anything suspicious.

He slipped into the shadows and pulled out his phone as he waited for the vehicle to come into sight. Moonlight caught the front of Caden's car. Reid let out a sharp huff of air. He was getting paranoid.

Reid walked up to his brother's car as Caden climbed out. "Where have you been?"

"Where do you think? Wedding plans. I tell you, I wish we would have eloped. To her credit, Gwen is doing everything fairly simply, but there are so many details you wouldn't believe, and now her aunt's here and wants to change things… If you ever find the right girl, convince her to elope."

"Seems like sound advice."

"I thought I'd stop by on the way home and make sure everyone was okay."

"I'm just out getting some fresh air."

"Is that all?"

"Claire and I were sitting out on the porch and winding down from a long day and… I don't know how it happened, but I kissed her."

"It doesn't sound like the worst thing that could happen."

"Mom ended up interrupting, but I don't think Claire is feeling what I am."

Caden followed him back toward the house and they sat down on the steps leading up to the front porch. The wind had picked up, but Reid barely felt it. "What are you feeling?"

"Confused, mainly. A part of me still feels so drawn to her."

"You do remember that you're the one who broke up with her."

Reid rested his elbows on his thighs and shook his head. "Of course I remember. And I've regretted it ever since."

"Have you thought about telling her that?" Caden asked.

"I don't think I should do that."

"Why not?"

"Because I never should have kissed her. No matter what happens, we're not getting back together. She made that very clear. Tonight was just… I don't know what tonight was other than a mistake, but it can't happen again. I can't let it because it won't work between us. I'm not going down that road again. And I need to respect her feelings."

"So you're just going to walk away. Like the last time."

"I don't know. If you would have told me two days ago that I'd be kissing Claire Holiday on my parents' front porch, I would have laughed you into the next county. But kissing her feels like Pandora's box has just been opened, and I'm now standing in the middle of this whirlwind, trying to find my balance."

"Listen…" Caden squeezed Reid's shoulder. "I know what it's like to have your heart broken. Cammie canceled our wedding the night before the ceremony because she'd fallen in love with someone else. And she never had the guts to tell me until then. I never imagined myself saying that in two weeks I'm getting married to the most beautiful, Godly woman I've ever met. Sometimes God gives you second chances. Sometimes He brings someone completely new into your life and rearranges it."

"I'm happy for you and Gwen. I really am." Reid tried unsuccessfully to shake off the frustration entangling him. "Something tells me Claire and I will never have that happy-ever-after ending."

Besides, what really mattered right now was finding out who was behind the threats on their lives. And after that, she'd be out of his life again for good.

TEN

Reid sat at the desk in the back corner of the police department, trying to stay focused on the computer screen in front of him. He had the list of the guests who had stayed at the B&B, and the video security footage to log in everyone who came and went. So far, nothing stood out to him.

He felt the familiar stir of his heart as he watched the video of Claire stepping in through the front door with her small suitcase, laughing about something Mr. Graham must have said. Why was it that no matter how much he tried to let go of her, reminders of her were suddenly all around him?

After an hour of watching the black-and-white footage, his vision was starting to blur. He pushed Pause and set down his pen before glancing across the room to where Claire was talking intently to the sheriff. He'd tried all morning to forget about what had happened between them the previous night, but the unexpected kiss had left him reeling. He'd dreamed about her during the night, and she was the first thing he'd thought about when he woke up, but he knew he was going to have to find a way to let her go, once and for all.

She'd been almost through eating by the time he got down to breakfast at his parents' house, and she'd been cordial, but distant. The ride to town had been more of the same. The barrier between him and her heart was a wall she had no plan to tear down. But surely that kiss had meant something to her. Hadn't it proven that they both had feelings, even if they didn't know how to deal with them? But what did that mean? She clearly had no desire to explore thoughts of getting back together.

And if he was honest with himself, she was right.

That kiss hadn't opened a door for them to consider exploring a relationship again. It had simply been an unexpected surge of emotion. Besides, he couldn't forget that in a couple of days she was going to be heading home, and he'd be here, living out his own life. The bottom line was that she wasn't a part of his life anymore.

He headed toward the coffee pot in the back of the room and grabbed himself a cup. Rubbing his neck, he slid into his seat again, then pushed Play on the video and continued looking through the footage, this time with the added boost of the caffeine. They needed to find a way to connect not only the fires, but also whoever had been after him and Claire. There had to be a link between the events, but he just couldn't figure out what it was.

He continued moving through the security footage, checking off guests and marking down the time on a pad of paper. A minute later he pushed Pause. The time code had jumped forward. Or had it? He checked again. There was no doubt about it. The numbers of the time stamp jumped forward again. Whoever had started that fire had managed to splice five minutes out of the surveillance video *and* had probably been in that house. But who? And how?

He scribbled down the time stamps on his log sheet. He needed to show Claire and get the footage to IT to see if they could retrieve the missing minutes. While he wasn't particularly tech savvy, he was pretty sure it was possible to retrieve what had been cut. Or at least he hoped so.

"Reid?"

Reid glanced up from his notes. "Hey, Shawn. What's up?"

"The captain sent me to bring over some files Claire had asked for, but she looks like she's pretty tied up."

"Thanks. I'll get them to her as soon as she's done. They've been in there at least forty-five minutes."

Shawn handed the files to Reid. "Are you finding anything?"

Reid hesitated. He trusted Shawn, but both the captain and the sheriff had been clear about keeping all information they gathered in a tight loop. The last thing they needed was for someone to speak out of turn and the details of the case to get leaked to the media.

"Still going through the footage."

Shawn sat down on the edge of the table.

"It's been nice to see Claire again, hasn't it?"

"It has."

"I heard that the two of you used to be quite an item."

Reid shook his head. "Whatever was between us all those years ago is long gone. For the moment it is just nice to catch up. But there isn't—won't be—anything more."

"You sound disappointed," Shawn said.

"It's just the way things are."

"I've seen her a couple times over the past few years

when I was up in Denver. It's great to see how much she's advanced with her career."

"Yes, it is. Seems like the sky's the limit for her."

"She's always been good at anything she does," Shawn said. "I was hoping she'd bring her son down here, though. I'd like to meet him."

Reid's mouth went dry. "Her son?"

"I think his name is Owen. I figured you knew she had a son."

"I... I didn't, actually, but I haven't seen her for years. Not since I left Denver. Like I said, we haven't kept in touch." Reid glanced toward the office where Claire was. "Are you sure she has a son?"

"Yeah, my mother told me about him. I think he's five. I remember my mom mentioned that he was a Christmas baby."

Shawn's words felt like a punch to the gut as Reid did the math. There had to be a mistake. It couldn't be his son. Could it? Claire would have told him. They'd made their mistakes, but she wouldn't have just gone and jumped into a relationship with someone else so quickly, would she?

"Reid...you okay?"

"Of course." He sat back, drumming his fingers against the desk. "Just tired from all that's been going on these past few days."

"I don't blame you."

Reid barely heard Shawn's reply. He had to be jumping to conclusions. If Claire had been pregnant when they broke up, she would have told him. Right?

Shawn slapped his thighs then stood up. "I need to head out, but if you would please give those to her once she's out of the meeting, I would greatly appreciate it."

"Of course. Not a problem."

"Listen, man," Shawn said, turning back to him. "I hope I didn't upset you. I just assumed you knew she had a son."

"It's fine. Claire has her own life to live. Whatever we had was over a long, long time ago."

"Okay then. I'll see you later."

Reid stared at the screen, but saw nothing. He needed to keep working on the footage to verify that there weren't any more holes. He was also going to have to talk with Claire, but it didn't make sense. If it were true, why hadn't she told him? She wouldn't have raised his child without telling him. Would she?

He'd heard news about her from time to time, but he'd never heard about her having a baby. Surely something like that would have trickled back to him. But on the other hand, they hadn't spoken for years, and when he'd left Denver, he'd lost contact with most people. So it was possible she'd had a child and he'd never found out. But again, why?

Ten minutes later, she came out of the office.

"Finding anything?" she asked.

Reid cleared his throat. "I did, actually. Still looking through the video footage, but I found a place where five minutes were cut."

"Wait…really?"

"Footage from the night you arrived."

"So someone could have entered the house and then somehow hacked in and sliced the footage, erasing their footprints?"

"That's what it's looking like. I'm verifying that's the only spot."

He'd answered her question, but his mind was on the dozen other questions he needed to ask her.

"So we're looking for an arsonist with hacking skills," she said. "We need to have someone see if they can find the missing footage."

"Agreed. Oh, and Shawn dropped these files off. Said you'd asked for them."

"Great. I did. Thank you."

He angled his chair around so he was facing her. "I know there's a lot going on right now, but can we take a walk? We need to talk."

"I told you I'd rather just forget about what happened last night—"

"This…this isn't about last night."

"Okay." The color seemed to drain from her face as she studied his expression. "Is everything all right?"

He caught her gaze and frowned. "That's what I need to find out."

Claire was already regretting her decision to talk with Reid. Somehow everything she'd convinced herself wouldn't happen had, and he'd become too much of a distraction. He'd kissed her, and if she were honest with herself, she'd wanted to kiss him, as well. He'd managed to stir everything up inside her that she'd thought was long buried. But while she'd persuaded herself that Reid no longer held a piece of her heart, that she no longer felt anything toward him, she'd been wrong.

It had been another hour before they'd been able to slip out of the police station to the small park with wooden benches a few hundred yards away. A thin layer of snow covered the ground along with the decorations put up every year, making the quiet spot look like a slice of winter wonderland. But all the red ribbons, lights and decorated wreaths couldn't fix what had gone wrong between them.

She sat down next to him on a bench overlooking the park, glad he'd chosen here instead of a restaurant. At least here they'd have more privacy, though sitting in a restaurant would have given her the distractions she needed.

"I turned the security footage in to the IT man," she said. "Hopefully he'll be able to find the erased footage and get us a close-up of our arsonist."

"That would be wonderful."

"We can also be fairly certain that it wasn't any of the regular guests. Though I don't want to assume anything, if it was one of them, they wouldn't have any reason to erase any of the footage, because they were supposed to be there."

"True. Except they might not want to be seen coming and going in the middle of the night." She swallowed hard, ready to get to whatever he'd brought her here to tell her. "I'm pretty sure you didn't ask to see me because you wanted to talk about the case. I really don't want something like this to come between us. I'd like—if possible—for us to at least remain friends."

"I am sorry about last night," Reid said. "And I just want to be clear that I wasn't trying to start anything between us. It took me by surprise."

"You don't have to apologize. I was taken off guard, as well. But the truth is, I'm not looking for a relationship."

Especially with you.

She fidgeted in her seat, suddenly feeling extremely awkward.

"I never was good at beating around the bush, so I'm just going to come out with it."

"Okay."

"Someone told me this morning that you have a child."

Nausea swept through her. This couldn't be happening. This…this wasn't how he was supposed to find out. If he ever did find out, she was supposed to be the one who told him. And now…and now it was too late.

"Claire." His fingers wrapped around her arm. "Are you okay?"

"Who told you?"

"Is it true?" he countered.

"Yes. His name is Owen, and he's turning five this month."

All the reasons her mother had used to convince her seemed to vanish. What had she been thinking all these years? She never should have kept Reid's son from him.

Silence hung between them as the seconds ticked by. But she couldn't talk. She could barely breathe.

"Is he mine?" Reid asked.

Claire searched for what to say. She'd rehearsed dozens of times telling him about Owen, but this…this wasn't one of the scenarios. She'd been foolish to think he wouldn't one day figure it out while she'd tried to bury her head in the sand and convince herself he'd never know.

"I'm sorry."

"You didn't answer my question, and I think I deserve to know the answer. Is Owen my son?"

"He is."

Reid stood, the veins on his neck pulsing as he started pacing in front of her. "I don't understand. Why didn't you tell me I had a son? Did you not know me well enough to know that I would have taken responsibility for him? Instead, you kept this to yourself. I don't understand."

His voice rose as he spoke, but she couldn't blame him.

What have I done, God?

But this wasn't God's fault. She'd made a mess, tried to fix it on her own and now she was going to have to pay the consequences.

"I wanted to tell you—"

"No." He turned back to her. "If you'd wanted to tell me, you would have. I can't believe you kept this from me, Claire. I have a son. *We* have a son. Don't you think that is something I would have wanted to know? And now he's turning five and I've never even met him. I didn't even know he existed. How could you do that to me?"

Tears streamed down her cheeks. "I don't know."

"Try. Please. At least try to explain."

"I… I planned to tell you, but you'd just broken up with me when I found out, and told me you weren't interested in marriage and a family." Claire was sobbing now. "I was convinced that I'd never know if you were staying with me because you loved me or out of a sense of duty."

"I'm just as responsible for what happened as you are. I wouldn't have walked out on you, Claire."

"But you already had."

He paused in front of her, then sat down. "I'm sorry."

Claire brushed away the tears that were spilling down her cheeks. "I wanted to pick up the phone a hundred times, but then Owen was born, and time passed, and the more time that went by, the harder it was to even think about calling and telling you."

"I want to meet him when this is over."

She nodded. "Of course, but I need to talk to Owen about you first."

"What have you told him about me?"

"He hasn't asked many questions yet, though I know the day is coming. Eventually I knew I would have to tell him the truth."

Her stomach cinched. She couldn't imagine what he was thinking at the moment. Guilt tangled up inside her and pulled tight. She wasn't surprised he wanted to see Owen, but then what? She couldn't expect this to end like some happily ever after fairy tale. He might have kissed her last night, but that had simply been because of lingering feelings that had not completely died out. And that wasn't going to be enough.

Reid clasped his hands in front of him and leaned forward. "I just wish… I wish you would have trusted me enough to tell me. To believe that I would have been there for you."

"I wanted you to love me because of who I was, not because of a sense of duty or responsibility."

He turned and caught her gaze. "But you didn't give me a chance. You made that decision for me. That was a decision only I could make."

Claire's phone rang and she pulled it out of her pocket, checking the caller ID. It was her mother. "I need to get this."

"Of course."

"Claire?"

"Mom…" Claire could tell her mother was crying. "What's wrong?"

There was a short pause on the line. "Claire… Owen's gone."

ELEVEN

Claire's hand shook as she hit Speaker so Reid could hear the call. Her mind fought to process the implications. This couldn't be happening. Not Owen…not her baby…he couldn't be missing. He was supposed to be with her mother. Safe.

"M-Mom… Mom slow down," Claire stuttered, her heart racing. "What happened?"

"We decided to have tacos for lunch at one of the food trucks. You know how much he loves those. I turned away for just a couple seconds to pay and then he was gone."

"Mom…he has to be there. He probably just wandered off. He's curious."

There had to be a reasonable explanation, something that could make sense out of this nightmare enveloping her.

"You don't understand, Claire. Someone took him. I saw them."

She saw them?

"Did you call the police?" Claire asked.

"Of course. I'm here at the station now, but Claire…"

Reid grabbed her elbow and steered her toward her car. "I'm driving you to Denver. Now."

"Who is that?" her mom asked.

"I'm with Reid. He'll drive me. Send me the address of the station. We'll be there as fast as possible."

As she followed Reid to the car, she thought how ironic it was that the father she'd kept from her child was now the one helping her find Owen. She never should have done this to Reid. It seemed so wrong now for her to have stolen that from him. But none of it mattered at the moment. The only thing that mattered was Owen.

Reid unlocked the vehicle, then quickly started the engine as she sat and buckled in.

"I'm sorry," she said.

"Forget about all of that for now. Let's just concentrate on finding our son."

Our son.

Her fingers pressed into the armrest as Reid peeled out of the parking lot and headed toward the highway.

"I know what you're thinking," he said.

"That this is somehow related to what is going on here? That this is all my fault?"

"Your fault? No. Why would this be your fault?"

"If someone's after me… Why didn't I realize they could get my family involved? I thought Owen would be safe. He's a hundred miles away and our arsonist… I thought our arsonist was here in town."

"I don't understand either, but there has to be a connection."

She picked up her phone and showed him her screen saver. "This is Owen."

Despite the anger she knew he had to feel, a smile crossed his lips. "He looks just like his mother."

"He's got his father's eyes." Her chest squeezed tighter. "What do they want, Reid? There haven't been any ransom demands yet. Or any threats. How can we fight someone when we have no idea who they are or what they want?"

He reached over and squeezed her hand. "I don't know, but I have no plans to lose my son just when I found him."

She started crying quietly as the reality of what had happened seeped through her. She couldn't breathe. Couldn't think. Couldn't imagine how terrified Owen had to be, wherever he was. She'd always hated leaving him, and rarely left him with anyone other than her mother, who'd always helped Claire navigate life as a single mom.

In fact, the only thing they'd really disagreed on was telling Reid. And while Claire ended up going along with her mother, she'd never been a hundred percent sure she was making the right decision. Weeks and months had gone by, though, and the more time that passed, the easier it had been to justify her decision. But now Reid knew, and she had no idea what he was really thinking. Or if he'd even had time to start processing what she'd told him.

She drew in a breath and pushed back the tears. She needed to do something tangible to keep her mind busy. If she didn't, she'd end up going mad.

"What would be the motivation for the arsonist to take him?" she asked Reid. For the moment, she was going to go with the assumption that the Rocky Mountain Arsonist was behind this.

"I've been asking myself the same question," Reid said. "I keep thinking about how some arsonists start fires for notoriety and a sense of control."

"That fits the profile."

"Even if their name isn't known, there's still the satisfaction of watching the fire burn on the television or at the scene. You've worked hard to keep these cases under the radar as much as you can, so the fires might not be getting the attention he or she wants. Think about how much news time a story would get if the lead arson investigator died in a fire set by the arsonist she's after. Or if her son was kidnapped. Both would hit the headlines."

Claire shuddered at the thought. It sounded impossible, but was it? Was this a situation where someone was angry because she was refusing to give him—or her—the airtime they wanted?

"What about the drone and your car flipping?" she asked. "I still can't see how it all fits together."

"I'm not sure, but it all has to be connected to the case."

"So someone is trying to get my attention." She stared out at the snow-covered ground and lines of trees. "If that's what they're shooting for, they're doing a pretty good job. I just wish they'd tell me what they want so at least I have something tangible to work with."

"I'm sorry. I can't imagine how difficult this is for you."

"It's the not knowing where Owen is that terrifies me. I just… I don't know how to feel, Reid."

"Tell me about Owen."

She let out a sharp breath at the shift in the conversation. More than likely it was because he truly wanted to know, but she also had a feeling he wanted to distract her. She owed him far more than just a description, but it was a start.

"He's never been big on toys, but he loves just hanging out with me or my mother. We love playing board games and reading together. He's into telling jokes—ones that don't always make sense, but that always make me laugh. This year we planted a garden in my mom's backyard and he had his own section because he wanted to grow tomatoes for pizza. He loves pizza. He has a bug collection, and a rock collection, and we try to go hiking or fishing as much as possible when the weather's good. I've promised him we'll ski for the first time this winter. I have a feeling he'll be outmaneuvering me before I know it. He also loves playing football, though I'm not sure when I'll be ready to get into the whole team experience."

"You're a great mom. I can tell."

"A great mom would tell the father he had a son."

"I'm not going to lie," he said, after a short pause. "I'm struggling with all of this and admittedly still pretty mad at you for not telling me. I feel like I've lost so much from not knowing the truth. But being angry at you isn't going to change anything. Especially right now. I just… I just hope you'll let me in your life now."

His words cut deep, but she couldn't blame him. "You have every right to be mad."

"Let's just focus on finding him. We'll have plenty of time later to figure out what this means and how this is going to work."

She studied his profile, his hands gripped tightly on the steering wheel, jaw tensed, brow furrowed. There was no way to go back and change the past, but maybe, just maybe, she'd been wrong and they could find a way to parent together.

And that might be what scared her the most—having Reid back in her life. She'd somehow convinced herself that he wouldn't care about Owen and telling him would simply make both their lives more difficult. Believing that had helped to ease her guilt when she'd clung to the idea that Owen didn't need a father in his life. At least, not one who didn't care about Owen. Sharing custody had always been her greatest fear, and not something she wanted for her son. He deserved a stable home, and yet she couldn't exactly run from the consequences of her decisions. She'd done that for far too long.

"I feel like I've created a mess," she said.

"We created a boy who needs us to love him. The rest will somehow fall into place."

She stared out the window, wishing he'd do anything but sit calmly next to her. It was a scene she'd played out in her mind over and over, but never under these circumstances, not in a nightmare where she lost Owen. And now they were going to have to do everything in their power to find their son.

Reid drove into the parking lot of the precinct in South Denver, then pulled into an empty parking space. Claire jumped out of the car before he'd even had a chance to turn off the engine. He quickly grabbed his phone and wallet and hurried after her, wishing he could help her more. But there was nothing he could say that could fix this. All he could do was pray that they find Owen.

Her son.

Their son.

Claire's mother was sitting in a back office of the station, waiting for them. The older woman looked a lot like her daughter, except for the additional hard lines around her mouth and eyes. If the reunion had been under different circumstances, he would have worried about her reaction to seeing him. Undoubtedly, the woman had never wanted him to be a part of her grandson's life and had been a vocal part in Claire's decision to keep him out of *her* life.

He breathed in the smell of coffee and felt his stomach turn. He hadn't even had time to wrap his head around the situation, but somehow the fact that their son was missing had managed to erase some of the anger he felt toward Claire. Not that he wasn't still mad at her for not telling him the truth earlier, but he knew he couldn't be focused on that right now. All that really mattered was finding Owen and catching whoever was behind this nightmare.

"Mom…" Claire pulled her mother into a hug, then stepped back between Reid and her mother. "You remember Reid."

"Of course." Anne Holiday wiped her puffy eyes. "It's been a long time."

He couldn't imagine what she had to be going through. While it wasn't her fault, the woman had to feel responsible for Owen's disappearance. He also knew she'd rather not be talking to him. It wouldn't matter to her that their mistakes had been consensual. Instead, he was the man who'd gotten her daughter pregnant. He shoved back the feelings and shook her hand.

"It's good to see you, though I wish the circumstances were different," he said.

"I wish they were different, as well." Her mother

pressed the back of her hand against her mouth, trying to push back sobs. "Claire… I'm so sorry. I don't know how this happened. When I went to grab us lunch, he was right behind me. Owen knows not to go anywhere with strangers, and yet… I don't know what happened. I turned around and he…he was getting into another vehicle. And I couldn't stop him."

Anne started sobbing again.

Claire pulled her mother against her. "It's not your fault, Mom. We're going to find him."

A detective walked up to them and cleared her throat. "I'm sorry to interrupt. I'm Detective Jennifer Kaufman. If the three of you will please take a seat at my desk…"

"I'm Claire Holiday, Owen's mother," Claire said as the three of them sat down at the cluttered desk in the back of the room. "This is Reid O'Callaghan. He's a friend from Timber Falls who drove me here. Tell me what we need to do to find my boy."

Reid's jaw tensed. He wanted to interrupt and say that he wasn't just a friend, but the father of the missing boy. Which sounded ridiculous. How could he have such strong feelings for a child he hadn't even known existed until a few hours ago?

"We're going to need to move as quickly as possible," the detective said, "but right now we don't have very much information other than what your mother was able to give me."

"Tell me what you need to know," Claire said. "We'll cooperate completely. Just please…tell us what we need to do to find my boy."

"Your mother said that Owen's father isn't in your

life," Detective Kaufman said. "Could this be a custody issue?"

"No, actually." Claire paused. "His father hasn't known about Owen."

The detective leaned forward. "You never told the father?"

Clare hesitated, glancing at Reid. "No. Not…not until today."

Reid's fingers gripped the sides of the chair he sat on. The room felt hot. Too hot. "I'm the father."

"You're Owen's father?"

Reid slipped off his jacket. "I am."

"And you just found out today?"

"Look, I get where you're going with all of this," Claire said, "but you're looking at the situation all wrong."

"She's right—" Reid started.

"Maybe, but the fact that a child goes missing the same day the father found out sounds…a bit off to me. Sounds very off, actually."

"Are you serious?" Claire said. "A little boy is missing. I'm telling you that his father—that Reid—had nothing to do with it. And there is no time to argue."

"Except that most children are taken by one of their parents in cases like this."

"Not this time." Claire pulled her badge out of her pocket and slammed it against the table. "Call my boss, or his, or both. I'm a fire inspector and have been working down in Timber Falls on a case. Reid O'Callaghan happens to work for the fire department there and has been helping with the case against the Rocky Mountain Arsonist. Right or wrong, we were split up right before I found out I was pregnant, and I chose not to tell Reid.

But Timber Falls is a small town and he found out, which was probably inevitable, but not until after Owen had already been kidnapped. The bottom line is that there's a very good chance my son is missing because of this arsonist, which makes finding him critical."

Detective Kaufman frowned. "I'll need their phone numbers to verify your story."

"Of course." Claire took the pen and paper the detective handed her and scribbled down the numbers. "Please hurry. I can assure you that Reid had nothing to do with it. We need to find Owen, which means focusing on the connection between my case and his disappearance."

"I'll be right back."

Claire nodded, then turned to Reid. "I'm sorry they think you're somehow involved in this."

"It's fine. They have to look at every angle."

"Yes, but they're wasting time."

Claire's mom leaned forward. "You told him? I don't understand."

"Someone else did, but that doesn't matter. Right now we need to focus on Owen." Claire clasped her fingers together. "You said you saw who took him?"

"When…when I turned around, he was getting into a brown sedan."

"And whoever took him? Did you see him?"

"Just his clothes. He was wearing jeans and a black sweatshirt. I didn't see his face. And the license plate was muddied."

Claire stood up and started pacing in front of the desk.

"I'm sorry, Claire."

"I know, it's just that this…this standing here and doing nothing. I can't do this."

Detective Kaufman sat back down at her desk. "Your story checks out."

"So you believe us now?" Claire asked.

"I have no reason not to."

Reid frowned. He had a feeling the woman wasn't at all convinced, but there was nothing else he could do to change her mind. At least not at the moment.

"We're going to need as much key information as you can give us," the detective said, "especially regarding the case you're working on and the possible connection. Your mother has already provided basics like Owen's weight, height, clothes he was wearing, identifying features, health issues and, of course, given us photos."

"What about an AMBER Alert?" Reid asked.

"Unfortunately we don't have very much information on the suspect or the suspect's vehicle, which is crucial in assisting the public. But, with the information you have just given me regarding the possible connection to the Rocky Mountain Arsonist, we believe that the child is in imminent danger, and thus we will be issuing an AMBER alert as well as entering him into the National Crime Information Center system."

Claire nodded. "Okay. What else?"

"We're going to need you to fill out some paperwork."

"Whatever you need."

Claire started writing the information on the forms given her while her mother spoke to another officer again. Reid sat across from Claire, feeling lost. He was Owen's father and yet he didn't know anything about the boy. He reached for a photo that had been printed off and ran his finger across the little boy's cheeks. He did have his mother's smile and his father's eyes. He'd told Claire he didn't think he'd ever have a family, but now he'd just found out he had a ready-made one.

Claire set down the pen and handed the detective the paperwork. "What do we do now?"

"I'm being assigned to your case," the woman said, "so I will give you my number so you can contact me. It's standard procedure to do a search of his room even though he disappeared outside his house. It will help us with fingerprints and DNA."

"Of course." A numbness swept through Claire. "Anything you want."

The detective scooted her chair back. "I know you believe that this is connected with a case you're working on, and we will certainly follow that lead, but we need to know if there is anyone who might have shown interest in your child lately."

"No. No one, but I can't just sit here. There's got to be more I can do."

"Polygraphs are standard procedure."

"Fine. I'm happy to take one."

"You might want to also talk about offering a reward, asking for help from friends and family to spread the word with a website and social media. The more people who see his face, the more chances that someone will spot him."

"Done."

"And I'll help, as well," Reid said, "with anything."

Claire nodded at him. "Thank you."

He caught the fear in her eyes. Fear of not knowing where Owen was. Fear that she might never see him again. Reid knew he couldn't understand everything that she was going through, but that didn't mean the situation didn't terrify him.

Reid's phone rang and he grabbed it out of his pocket. "I need to get this."

He stood up and moved away from the desk a few feet.

"Griffin, what have you got?"

"Couple things. One, we found the truck that hit you and were able to pull a couple partial prints off, but the reality of getting a match is a long shot."

"A long shot is better than nothing at this point."

"Second, they were able to get some of the missing footage off the security camera from the B&B. The cameras caught a two-second clip of someone leaving through the back door. Once the fire started it's pretty clear what happened, when you combine Mike's testimony with the physical evidence."

"Which means we have footage of our suspect."

"Yes," Griffin said, "but once again, it's not going to be easy to ID him. The footage is grainy and there isn't a clear shot of his face."

"Can you send me what you've got? Maybe Claire will be able to recognize him."

"It's possible," Griffin said. "In the meantime, I'm sorry I missed you. I got your message that you needed to talk."

Reid moved farther out of earshot to the window overlooking the back parking lot.

"Reid?"

"Sorry… What I need to say really needs to be said in person, but I'm here in Denver and…" Reid hesitated.

"What's going on?"

"I just found out that Claire has a son."

There was the expected silence while Griffin took in the news.

"A son? Okay…well, that's a surprise."

"That's not the real news. I also found out that I'm the father."

"Wow… I have to say that isn't what I was expecting to hear."

"Me neither, but he's missing, Griffin."

"Missing?"

"Yes." Reid rubbed the back of his neck, forcing himself to stay calm while his heart raced. "We think it's related to the case she's trying to solve."

"The Rocky Mountain Arsonist? You've got to be kidding."

"I wish I was."

"Where are you right now?" Griffin asked.

"At a police station here in Denver. We've been meeting with a detective who deals with missing people, though you can imagine who's top of the suspect list."

"I'm afraid I can. What can I do?"

"At this point, I don't know…" Voices raised behind him, and he shifted his attention toward the commotion. "Hang on, Griffin. I'm going to need to call you back."

"Give me an update as soon as you know something."

"I will." Reid hung up the call and shoved the phone into his back pocket. "Claire… Claire, what's going on?"

"We have a possible sighting of your son," Detective Kaufman said.

"Where?"

"Someone called in and told us they'd seen a child matching Owen's description about forty minutes south of here near one of the cabins. The couple didn't think anything about it until they saw his photo and recognized him."

"He was alone?" Reid asked.

"They didn't see anyone else with him, but we can't confirm that."

Reid picked up his coat off the back of the chair, feeling the urgency pressing against his chest. "Let's go."

TWELVE

Claire glanced at the dashboard from the passenger seat of her car for the hundredth time in the past forty-five minutes. Two o'clock. She pressed her lips together. Every minute that passed was another minute Owen's life was in danger, another minute she wasn't with her son. She'd convinced her mother to partner with a friend from their church who'd promised to help set up a social media presence and get the word out that Owen was missing. An AMBER alert had been issued. Local law enforcement had all been notified and Owen's photo distributed. But what if everything they were doing wasn't enough to find him?

It still seemed ironic that it was Reid who sat next to her in the driver's seat as they searched for Owen. And while Reid might never have met Owen, the tension he felt was palpable. His jaw was taut and his grip on the steering wheel tight, his frustration clearly as much with her as it was with the situation. Which was why they hadn't really said anything to each other since leaving the police station.

But what was she supposed to say?

If she could take back hiding Owen from Reid, she knew now that she'd have already done it in a heartbeat.

But it was too late for do-overs.

"According to the GPS, we're five minutes out," Reid said, turning off the main road onto a dirt lane.

Five minutes.

She nodded, wishing her heart would stop pounding and her mind would stop racing. She still couldn't fully take in what was going on. What if another five minutes was going to be five minutes too late?

She pushed away the thought as Reid pulled in next to the string of cars behind the cabin where Owen had been spotted. She jumped out of the car, searching for Owen as she hurried to where Detective Kaufmann stood talking to a uniformed officer.

"Did they find them?"

The detective turned to her and frowned. "Local PD have done a sweep of the cabin and the immediate area, but there is no sign of him yet. I'm sorry—"

"We need to expand the search," Claire said.

"Unfortunately, we have no evidence that he was even here."

Claire took a step back, her mind spinning, as Reid moved next to her. She couldn't deny that that woman was right. It was possible that their witness hadn't really seen Owen. It could have just as easily been some other little boy playing outside their family's cabin.

"Who's staying here?" Claire asked. She might not be a detective, but her role as fire inspector had trained her to know how to conduct an investigation.

"An older couple on vacation," Detective Kaufman said. "They claim they haven't seen Owen or any children hanging around here, for that matter, but they've been inside all day, so it's possible he was here and they missed him."

"And you're sure this is the cabin where he was spotted?"

Detective Kaufman nodded. "I'm sorry."

But that would lead them back to square one with no idea where Owen might be.

"I found this back behind the cabin, under some snow." One of the uniformed officers approached them, carrying a blue knit beanie with a red stripe.

Owen's cap.

She grabbed the beanie and turned it inside out, looking for the tag she'd sewn on it so he wouldn't lose it at preschool.

Owen Holiday.

She pulled the hat to her chest. "This is Owen's. He was here."

But where was he now?

"We're already canvasing the area for witnesses, but houses are spread out here, and most people are inside because of the cold."

Claire turned slowly, studying the thick tree line around them. What had Owen been doing here? Who had brought him here? And where was he now? Nothing made sense.

"Claire?"

She felt Reid's hand on her arm. "I'm fine. We need to expand the search. He has to be nearby."

"She's right," Detective Kaufman said. "But we've got less than two hours until dark. We'll pair up and search these woods. You can get your assignment from me, and I'll hand out radios to each team. He was spotted outside a cabin, alone, so we're going to assume he walked out of here. People—even kids—tend to stay on trails, so we'll start there. We'll branch off and search a perimeter of trails. If we still don't find him, we'll widen the search even further. Are the two of you okay together?" the detective asked.

"Of course," Reid said.

Claire caught Reid's expression as the detective handed them the radio. She had no idea now why she'd thought that Reid would want nothing to do with her or Owen. Or why she'd kept such a huge secret from him for all this time.

"Be extra careful out there. I spent some time on the phone with Captain Ryder, who explained more of the situation to me. Since we still don't know who has been targeting the two of you, I want you to be extra vigilant. And while I'd like to keep you both locked up in protective custody for safekeeping, I have a six-year-old little girl. There's no way I'd not be involved in a search if she went missing."

"Thank you."

"We'll be fine," Reid said. "Our only focus at the moment is finding Owen."

"Just stay in radio contact and you should be fine. We're going to find him."

A truck pulled up with three firefighters from Timber Falls, including Shawn, as Claire and Reid headed toward their assigned trail.

"We got permission to help with the search," Shawn said, walking up to the detective.

"Captain Ryder told me you were coming," Detective Kaufman said. "We'll get you set with radios and a map right away."

Claire waved her thanks as she and Reid headed off, grateful for the show of support.

"The detective's right, you know," Reid said. "We're going to find him."

Claire silently walked beside Reid through the woods down the trail leading south away from the cabin, praying he was right. Panic bubbled inside her as her feet crunched on the dry pine needles. They might still have a couple of more hours of light left, but before long the sun would shift behind the mountains and the temperatures would begin to drop. She had no idea if Owen was by himself out here or locked up somewhere. And either scenario horrified her. She pulled her pink scarf tighter around her neck. How had they gotten here?

Someone had taken her son.

She didn't know what they wanted or how long it was going to take to find him. Or if she was ever going to see Owen again.

She scanned the tree line surrounding her, looking for any movement. The not knowing was more terrifying than anything else. Working as a firefighter, she'd seen the devastation when someone lost a loved one in a fire. The truth was, they had no idea where Owen was. The beanie could be nothing more than a false lead, but nothing was going to stop her from turning over every stone until she found her son.

"Why would he have been out here alone?" Claire asked, knowing she was asking questions Reid couldn't answer. "Did he run away and escape from the arsonist? Or maybe, for whatever reason, the arsonist just left him here."

But why? Nothing made sense.

"I wish I could answer. Does Owen like hiking?"

"We've done quite a lot of short hikes, mainly trails around Denver. Places like Lookout Mountain and Golden Gate Canyon State Park." She buttoned the top of her coat in an attempt to block the wind. "I taught him what to do if he got lost, that he needed to stop walking, stay put and make a lot of noise so people could hear him."

But if he'd escaped and someone was chasing him?

She'd thought she'd done everything right. How could things have suddenly gone so wrong?

"This isn't your fault," he said, as if he could read the guilt she was feeling. "None of this is."

"But this is different, Reid. He isn't just a five-year-old lost in the woods, trying to get home. Someone took him and we can't just assume that whoever did is gone. They could have moved him. He could be miles from here by now."

"Or he could be right here somehow. We're not going to stop looking until we find him."

Panic built in her chest until she could barely breathe, as they called out his name. *This* was every parent's worst nightmare. And, somehow, she'd just gotten caught up in the whirlwind. How was she supposed to deal with this when terror was messing with her ability to cope? Reid stopped beside her, then flashed his light into the brush toward an outcropping of moss-covered rocks.

"Did you see something?" she asked.

"I'm not sure. Just a flash of color."

Her heart stopped as she searched the rocky landscape. Her mother had dressed Owen in a black T-shirt, jeans, his red jacket and his favorite beanie. Now, without his beanie, she was worried he was going to be too cold.

God please... I know none of this took You by surprise, but I don't know how to deal with losing my son. And if we don't find him...

Reid moved off the trail while she stayed a few steps behind him. He bent down, then held up a hat. "Sorry. Someone lost a hunting hat."

It wasn't Owen.

She fought back the tears. She was supposed to be the strong one when it came to responding to an emergency. But this...this was unraveling her. The fact that they would involve her son. And then there was Reid. She couldn't even imagine what he thought about her, but for the moment, their only focus was finding Owen.

Her child.

Their child.

She glanced at Reid, feeling the tension that had settled between them continue to tighten as they kept walking. She knew he was going to need time to work through the shock of the situation, but this...this silence between them was deafening.

How had it come to this? Had she really thought she was going to go the rest of Owen's life without Reid ever finding out? Guilt that she'd shoved away for so long engulfed her. But try as she might, this wasn't something she could take back or change. God might be able to redeem the irredeemable, but she would have to carry the guilt of what she'd done for the rest of her life.

The crack of a gunshot echoed around them. Reid stumbled beside her. She reached out to grab him as she tried to discern where the shot came from.

"Reid..."

"I think I was hit."

* * *

Adrenaline surged as Reid struggled to keep his balance. He searched the surrounding forest for movement. His brain struggled to connect the dots, but the shot he'd heard had been followed by a searing pain in his side.

She wrapped her arm around him. "We need to get to cover. Now."

Reid leaned against her as she pulled him toward an outcropping of rocks, pain shooting through him with each step. "I don't think it's serious."

"If you were shot, it's serious. You're probably in shock." She helped him lean back against the rock, then crouched next to him, and pulled out her radio. "Shots fired in grid two. I repeat, shots fired."

The radio crackled. "Roger that. We're tracing your phone's GPS for your location."

"Reid's been shot."

"Sending backup your way now. Stay down and out of sight. Do not engage. I repeat, do not engage."

Reid struggled to get up, despite the order. "We need to find out where the shooter is."

"Stop." She pushed against his shoulders. "Did you not just hear what he said?"

"He's still out there, Claire, and he can't be far. Besides, we're sitting ducks here."

"That might be true, but neither of us are armed. And on top of that, I can't have you bleeding out in front of me. It's hard to see, but I need to see how bad it is."

Reid nodded, wincing at the pain.

She ran her hand across his side, then pulled back his coat. "You're bleeding and your shirt is sticking. I'll be as careful as I can."

This couldn't be happening. Owen was missing, but the arsonist's objective had to be bigger. Reid watched her work, hating that he felt so vulnerable—that they both were so vulnerable. Because no matter how angry he was at Claire for what she'd done, he didn't want anything to happen to her or Owen.

She aimed the phone's flashlight closer to him as she examined his side.

"How bad is it?" he asked.

"From what I can see, it looks as if the bullet skimmed across your rib cage."

"Then I'll be fine." He grabbed her wrist with his good hand. "We need to find whoever's out there."

"Forget it. You're not going anywhere. Whoever is out there is armed and looking for us." She pulled away from him, took off her scarf and wrapped it around him. "I need you to press this tightly against your side. It's not bad, but it is bleeding."

He caught her expression and knew, like him, she wasn't simply thinking about sitting around and waiting. "You're not going out there?"

"I am, and you can't stop me. Whoever shot you could find us before help gets here. You said it yourself. We're sitting ducks."

"Claire…please. We'll do what they said. Backup will be here in a couple minutes."

She crouched down next to him and caught his gaze in the fading light. "I'm not going far, but the last thing we need is another ambush while you're down."

He tried to get up, but another sharp stab of pain followed. He bit the edge of his lip. The bullet might have just skimmed him, but it felt like his side was on fire. "Don't go. Promise you'll wait here for the cavalry to arrive."

She pressed her lips together.

"Promise me, Claire."

She nodded.

"This was a setup. He's out there, searching for us now. This wasn't just about Owen. It's still about us, somehow, and the investigation." Reid kept his voice low as he searched the thick woods for any signs of movement, but all he could see were branches, rustling in the breeze. "A second shot and he might not miss his target. All we have to do is lay low. Help is coming."

"What about Owen? Reid, if anything happens to him…"

She was crying silently next to him. He could hear her breath coming in uneven spurts as she tried to hold back, but already tears were streaming down her face.

He grabbed her hand. "Deep breaths, Claire. Slow, deep breaths. We're going to find Owen. We're going to be okay."

"I'm sorry. You're the one injured, and I'm the one freaking out on you."

"It's fine. You have every reason to feel panicked. And I'm sorry. I truly am."

"Me too." She took in another ragged breath. "Though, if I didn't know better, I'd say you were a bit accident prone."

"Seriously? You're going to go there?"

She cocked her head, still keeping her voice low. "With your wrist brace and now my pink scarf wrapped around your side."

"Please." Reid shook his head. "Don't make me laugh. It hurts."

"I'm sorry." She shot him an impish grin, allowing some of the tension between them to lessen. "If I don't laugh, I'm going to completely lose it."

"I know."

A scattering of memories, buried years ago, shot to the surface. She'd always been able to make him laugh. It was something he'd loved about her—the ability she had to never take things too seriously and to always see the silver lining in a situation, no matter how bad. But today, finding good in any of this seemed impossible. There were too many unknowns, too many disconnected parts, and he had no idea how to bring order to what was happening around them. Even firefighting had specific techniques they used to get in control and stay in control while knocking down a blaze.

But this…he had no formula to combat this.

"I don't know how to deal with this. I can't face life without Owen."

He took her hand and squeezed it. "You're not going to have to. We'll find Owen and whoever is behind this."

"I keep praying, but the arsonist… I don't know what they want or who they are, but there has to be an end to it, Reid."

"We're in this together now. Owen's out here and we're going to find him."

He wanted to promise her that everything was going to be okay. They'd find Owen, and then the three of them could find a way to make things work. He pulled his gaze away from her. As much as he'd tried to fight it, he couldn't deny that so many of the feelings he'd had for her all those years ago had never gone away. But the fact that she'd never told him about Owen… how was he supposed to forget that? How was he supposed to forgive her for that? He wasn't even sure it was possible. In order for things to work, he would have to trust her again, but he wasn't sure that was something he could do.

The snap of a branch jerked him out of his thoughts.

Claire started to stand up.

He pulled on her arm with his good hand, keeping her down. "Claire...don't."

"I won't go far. I promise. I just need to see what's out there."

She grabbed a thick branch off the ground, then moved to the edge of the rock, despite his protests.

"It's our backup, Reid," she said a few seconds later.

Reid blew out a sigh of relief as two men in uniform hurried toward them.

"He's been shot," Claire said, "but it's just a graze."

"We've got all the teams searching for the shooter. We know he's out there and we will find him. It's just a matter of time."

"But how?" she asked. "We don't even have a description of our suspect."

"True, but we do have good news. We just got an update. They found Owen."

THIRTEEN

"They found him?" The news slammed through Claire like a freight train.

Oh God, please, please let Owen be okay.

"Tell me he's not hurt."

"From what I understand, he's fine," the shorter of the two officers said. "He was found about a quarter of a mile from here at a cabin, straight back up this trail and to the left. A couple of the firemen from Timber Falls found him sitting on the porch, playing video games. Apparently he'd been told to stay put."

"I don't understand." Claire's mind fought to take in the details. "Why would someone take him, then leave him alone?"

"I wish I could tell you more, but I don't have any other details. I'm sorry. I know Detective Kaufman is wanting to ask him some questions and hopefully get some more information, but for the moment let's just get you back to him."

"We've got an ambulance on the way," the second officer said as he helped Reid onto his feet. "Can you walk?"

"My side still feels like it's on fire, but yeah… I can walk."

The hike back up the tail seemed to take forever with Reid's injury slowing them down. She glanced back at him, knowing he was in pain, but at the same time feeling the urgency to get to Owen.

"Please don't get too far ahead, ma'am. We have to assume we still have an active shooter out here."

She knew their advice was sound, but she needed to see for herself that not only had they found Owen, but that he was really okay. An event like this was going to be traumatic, no matter what he'd gone through. She picked up her pace, leaving Reid and the two officers trailing behind her. She never should have left him, never should have put her job above his safety. She should have known that if she was a target, then he could be, as well.

This isn't your fault.

Reid's words came rushing back at her. Guilt, though, had become a constant companion over the past few years. Guilt over not telling Reid about Owen. Guilt knowing she'd deprived Reid of his son and his parents of their grandchild. Shedding that guilt wasn't something she was good at.

She turned left at the trailhead, then started running when she caught sight of several officers standing outside one of the cabins that were scattered through this area. Owen was sitting on the front porch with a uniformed officer standing next to him. Someone had wrapped a blanket around him. With darkness quickly falling, he had to be freezing, with no hat and no gloves. Claire ran up the wooden stairs and pulled him into a hug.

"Mom...you're squishing me."

"I'm sorry." She set him back down on the padded

chair where he'd been sitting, then crouched down in front of him. "I was worried about you. Are you okay?"

"I'm fine. I had some hot chocolate with marshmallows." Owen's brow furrowed. "But I was worried. The man told me you were hurt."

She glanced up at the detective. "What do you mean, Owen?"

"He said he was going to take me to you. That you were in an accident and we needed to hurry."

Claire pressed her lips together. There were so many things she wanted to ask him. Like why he'd gotten into the car of a stranger. Why he hadn't run back to her mom when approached so none of this would have happened.

"Mom? Are you okay?"

"I'm fine, baby." She brushed back his bangs. "As long as you're okay, I'm fine."

Owen cocked his head. "So you really weren't hurt?"

"No. I promise."

"I'm glad." He pulled her into a hug, melting away all the frustration she was feeling. All that mattered was that he was safe and with her now. Nothing was going to diminish that.

"I'm glad too." Claire rocked back on her heels.

"I want you both inside while we look for our shooter," Detective Kaufman said, motioning them into the cabin.

"Of course." Claire sat down on a worn couch next to Owen in the cozy living room. "Do you know where the man is that took you?"

Owen shrugged. "He said he was going to get you and bring you here. He made me promise that I would wait here, but he let me play with this game. But then he didn't come back, and I was starting to get cold."

She tugged the blanket tighter around his coat. "Well, this blanket should warm you up."

"Do you think I can have some more hot chocolate?"

Claire wiped the tears away from her cheeks, then laughed. "I'm sure we can find you some hot chocolate once we leave here."

"Mom..." Owen leaned forward, cupping her face with his hands. "I didn't mean to make you cry."

Claire swallowed the lump in her throat. "I know you didn't, baby."

"And I know I'm never supposed to talk to strangers, but he said you were hurt."

"This isn't your fault, Owen. None of this is your fault. I just missed you very much."

"I missed you too."

As much as she wanted to snatch him up and leave, pretending none of this had happened, she knew they needed answers. Whoever had taken Owen and shot Reid was somewhere nearby. "Do you know where the man is? The man who brought you here?"

Owen shook his head. "He just told me he was going to get you. Told me I needed to stay right here, and he would bring you to me."

Shawn stepped into the cabin.

"That's the man who found me," Owen said, a smile back on his face.

"How are you doing, buddy?" Shawn asked. "I wanted to check on the two of you before the guys and I head back to Timber Falls."

"He seems fine." Claire stood, keeping her hand on

Owen's shoulder. "We both are now. And Shawn, I owe you for finding my boy. Thank you so much."

"Of course. We were just doing the sweep of our section and found him sitting here. I'm just glad he's safe. Glad this is over."

"So am I, but we still need to find our arsonist, but we found Owen, and that's all that matters for the moment."

Shawn shoved his hands into his back pockets. "So you think this is connected to the Rocky Mountain Arsonist?"

"I do."

Reid walked in behind Shawn, shifting Claire's attention. Her heart stirred. No matter what had happened between them over the past few hours, no matter how hard she fought it, there was a part of her heart that would always be his.

"We just heard you were shot, but didn't get any details," Shawn said.

"I'll live. Thankfully, it was just a graze."

"Have the paramedics checked it out?" Claire asked.

"Not yet. I wanted to make sure Owen was okay first."

"He is." Claire tousled Owen's hair. This wasn't how she'd ever pictured the two of them meeting. But they were both okay, and at the moment that was really all she cared about.

Claire nodded her thanks to Shawn, then turned back to her son. "Owen... I want you to meet someone else. This is Reid O'Callaghan. He and I used to be friends a long time ago."

"It is very nice to meet you, Owen," Reid said.

Owen held out his hand and shook Reid's. "Are you a fireman like Mr. Shawn?"

"I am."

"I think I wanna be a fireman when I grow up."

"I have a feeling you'll make a great fireman."

"Well, I have to grow up first."

Reid chuckled. "That's true."

"Is that my mom's scarf?" Owen asked.

"It is."

"You got shot?"

"It's just a scrape," Reid said. "Your mom patched me up."

"She's good at stuff like that."

"Yes, she is."

Claire glanced at Reid, then Owen, then back to Reid again while the two of them kept talking. It was uncanny the similarities she saw in father and son. At some point, she was going to have to tell Owen the truth. Hopefully, he'd forgive her for not telling him sooner. But that wasn't something she could worry about today.

Detective Kaufman came in from one of the bedrooms. "Claire… Reid… I need the two of you to look at something we just found."

"I can wait here with Owen," Shawn said.

"I…" Claire hesitated, not wanting Owen out of her sight.

"We'll be right here," Shawn said. "He'll be fine. I promise."

Claire knelt down in front of Owen. "The detective needs to show me something, but I'll be right back. Shawn is an old friend. He'll wait here with you."

"Okay."

Claire hesitated, trying to convince herself not to worry, then followed Detective Kaufman into the bedroom where two other officers were standing, including Griffin O'Callaghan.

"Griffin," Reid said, walking toward his brother. "I didn't know you were here."

"This cabin is under our jurisdiction, so we were called in." Griffin's gaze dropped to the pink scarf and the bloodstain. "Reid…what happened?"

"It's just a graze. I'll be fine."

"A graze? I heard there had been shots fired, but I didn't realize—"

"I'm fine. Really."

"Maybe, but you still need to have someone look at it," Claire said.

"And I will. But first, what's going on?"

Griffin hesitated, apparently not convinced his brother should be there. "We've got teams searching now for the shooter, but I thought you'd want to see this. The room was locked when we got here."

The room was decorated simply, with just a bed, a dresser and a desk. But it was the desk covered with stacks of papers and photos that caught her attention. Behind it was a bulletin board filled with more black-and-white photos.

"I don't know as much as you do about the Rocky Mountain Arsonist, but I'm pretty sure these are all pictures of the related fires," Griffin said.

"And over here," Detective Kaufman said, "there are a dozen lighters on the dresser."

Claire walked across the room to the desk, fighting back nausea. There was no doubt that this was connected and they'd found their arsonist, but there was one thing that terrified her more than anything else. Owen had been here, at this cabin, with a murderer.

* * *

"Claire?" Reid stepped up beside her. "What do you think?"

"Griffin's right." Her hand shook as she pulled on a glove Griffin handed her, then picked up one of the photos. "These photos are definitely from the fires we've been investigating," Claire said. "I recognize them. Breckenridge, Aspen, Montrose… It looks like our arsonist has been using this house as a base."

Photos of the remains of a dozen burned buildings were pinned to a bulletin board. News articles had been printed off and clipped together, and there was another pile of printouts that looked like reactions to the fires on social media.

"What's the point, though?" Reid asked. "Why would he keep them?"

"Some kind of trophy?" Griffin asked.

Claire nodded. "That would make sense. He didn't find the notoriety he craves on the local news or online, but this way, he has photos of what he's destroyed. It gives him the illusion of power and control over the situation."

Mixed with photos of the burning buildings were photos of the crowds.

"Some of these look familiar. Some of them I haven't seen," Claire said. "We dug up as many photos and videos on social media as we could. There was a man in a hoodie we believe to be the same person, but we were never able to get a clear enough photo to ID him."

"We found a printer, but no computer," Detective Kaufman said.

"What if he's in these photos?" Griffin asked.

"It's possible, but we've gone through the photos we have over and over and so far never found a connection between the different fires other than the lighters that were left at the scene and the way the fires were started."

Reid studied the photos on the bulletin board. Unless he—or she—was in disguise.

"Reid…" Claire held up another photo. "These aren't just from the fires. Apparently our fire-spitting drone also took pictures. And it looks like there are more from the fire at the B&B—"

"And from the scene of my wreck."

Reid felt his mouth go dry. There was a stack of images of the two of them out on horseback, taken from the drone. He turned back to the desk, wincing at the pain that shot through him. He'd run into burning buildings to save people, but had never been targeted himself. And what made it even more unsettling was that he had no idea why.

"What are you thinking?" Claire asked.

Reid rubbed the back of his neck, trying to put everything together, but the pieces still didn't fit. "I'm just trying to make sense of all of this. He uses this as his base, documents everything he does, including his attacks on us, then brings your son here. What does he want? Is it just a game he gets pleasure from, or does he actually have an end goal?"

"That's what we need to figure out," Claire said.

"Who owns this cabin?" Reid asked.

Detective Kaufman pulled out her notes. "A Mr. and Mrs. Fuller, but it sounds like they're only here a couple weeks out of the year in the summer."

"So our arsonist was squatting here and keeping records of everything he did, anything related to the fires that he could get his hands on," Griffin said. "We can bring in a forensics team and sweep the place, see if we can get some fingerprints. Hopefully, we'll come up with answers soon, but there's no question any longer that the two of you need to be in protective custody."

"I can't run this case while hiding," Claire said.

"I'm not asking you to drop the case, but you have a son out there who needs you, Claire. We can find a way for you to continue working on the case without putting your lives in danger."

Reid caught the conflict in her eyes, but still knew her well enough to know she'd always choose her son over her career. And as angry as he felt toward her, she was the kind of person who'd always kept her priorities straight. But that didn't mean she wouldn't try to find a way to work outside the box.

"You're right. I need to be with my son, but I also need to find a way to catch whoever's behind this. No one can guarantee Owen's safety until then."

"Why don't you come back to the ranch, both of you?" Griffin said. "You and Owen will be safe there, and your mother can come, as well, if that would make you feel better. I know for sure that you don't need to be investigating out in the field. I'll have CSI sweep this place and gather all evidence and get it to you. Agreed?"

Reid nodded. "I'll help you go through everything, Claire. We're going to find who's behind this. There has to be evidence here. No one is infallible. Between the photos, the lighters and the social media downloads, we're going to find something that identifies whoever is setting these fires."

"I can agree to that."

"Good, then it's settled."

Reid hesitated, searching her face. He had so many questions he wanted to ask her. He hated the fact that this case had to take priority right now, but whatever needed to be said between the two of them was going to have to wait. Keeping their son safe was all that really mattered.

"Why don't you go get Owen?" Griffin turned to Claire. "I'll escort you to my truck while Reid gets checked out by the paramedics. Then we'll get all three of you out of here and to the ranch."

Reid nodded, but he was still uneasy about the situation. Whoever was behind this had resources and didn't seem to have limits to what they did. The attacks had taken place both at the ranch by the drone and in broad daylight on the highway. What if their plan wasn't enough to keep Claire and Owen safe?

Griffin laid a hand on Reid's shoulder. "You don't seem convinced with the plan moving forward."

"I am. It's just…" He glanced at Claire, who was asking the detective a question. There probably wasn't any plan he'd be happy with. He wasn't just worried about an old girlfriend. All of this had taken a very personal twist. His son's life was in danger.

"We need to figure out who's behind this as soon as possible."

Griffin nodded. "I know this is important to you, and we will. I promise."

They headed back into the living room behind the women. Claire stopped short in front of him.

"Owen…"

"What's wrong?" Griffin asked.

Reid glanced at the spot where they'd left their son with Shawn. A shot of terror flooded through him. Owen was gone.

FOURTEEN

The panic that had tortured her all day raised its ugly head again.

"Where's Owen? He was just right here…with Shawn."

This couldn't be happening. She never should have let him out of her sight again. This was where the arsonist had brought her son, which meant he had to be nearby, and now, if he'd managed to grab her son again…

"Owen?" She shouted louder this time as she ran outside onto the porch.

"Claire?" Shawn turned around. Owen stood next to him on the corner of the porch.

"Mom, are you okay?"

"Owen…" She picked him up and held him against her chest.

"Mom."

She put him down, but didn't let go of his hand.

"I'm sorry," Shawn said. "We just stepped out onto the porch. I thought it would be safe with so many officers out here. The sheriff is taping this off as a crime scene and Owen wanted to watch. I told you I'd take care of him for you."

"I know. I shouldn't have panicked."

"No, I don't blame you," Shawn said. "We should have stayed in the cabin. I wasn't thinking. And you've already been through so much today. I really am sorry."

Detective Kaufman walked up to them. "And I'm sorry to interrupt, but we are going to need to talk to Owen and see if he can give us any clues to who took him. And while I'd like to work on your timetable, the sooner the better. We need to find this man, and Owen has been with him."

"Of course," Claire said. "I understand."

"We're actually not far from Timber Falls, and I have colleague there who's a psychologist and has worked with the police before. If it's okay with you, we can go there immediately." Detective Kaufman lowered her voice. "I also need to be mindful of your son."

Claire pulled the detective a couple of feet away, but kept Owen in full view. "I agree that the sooner we find this person, the sooner this will all be over. I'm just worried about him. He doesn't seem to understand the significance of what happened. I don't know the best way of handling things, but I don't want him to feel as if he's in trouble."

"I understand. Stacy is good at uncovering details without making him feel guilty or scared." Detective Kaufman glanced at her watch. "I'm going to keep the teams searching for now, but I'll have Deputy Griffin escort you back to Timber Falls."

Thirty minutes later, Claire was sitting in a back room of the Timber Falls sheriff's office, handing Owen a mug of hot chocolate with marshmallows someone had scrounged up for him. She'd asked Reid to come, as well, knowing that despite what they might feel toward each other, they had to put Owen and finding his kidnapper first.

Claire sat. "Owen, I'd like you to meet someone. Her name is Miss Porter."

"Hello."

"I'm happy to meet you, Owen. You can call me Miss Stacy if you'd like."

Owen just nodded.

"Sweetie, I'll be right here the whole time, but Miss Stacy would like to talk to you about the man who took you. And when you're done talking with her, I thought we might go get some tacos."

"Okay."

"Just answer everything she asks you as best you can."

Claire glanced at Reid before leaning back in her chair, hating how out of control she felt, how hard it was to not take over the conversation.

"It sounds like you've had quite an exciting day," Stacy said.

"Yep."

"Can we talk about it?"

"I guess."

"What can you tell me about the man in the brown car?"

Owen took a sip of his hot chocolate. "I was waiting for my grandma. He told me my mom was hurt and he was going to take me to see her. Told me my grandma would come after she bought lunch. That it was important that we hurry."

"Is that why you went with him?"

"Yes. But I don't know why he told me that. My mom said she's fine."

"You know, Owen, I'm not sure why he said that, either, but I know that your mother and the others are doing everything they can to find out. But mainly they are just happy you are safe. It's always scary for a mommy when she doesn't know where her child is."

"I was scared too."

"Owen, we want to find the man so we can talk to him, but we really need your help."

Owen shifted in his seat. "Would that mean I'm like a sheriff's deputy?"

"I bet if you help me, we could find you a badge. Would you like that?"

Owen nodded.

"Good. Now, do you remember what the man looked like?"

"Not really. He had a mask on. Well…kind of a mask."

"What do you mean, Owen?"

"He had a hat and glasses and a beard. But it wasn't a real beard though."

Claire fiddled with the zipper of her jacket, praying he'd be able to give them something concrete, but five-year-olds were more interested in fast food and video games than remembering a description.

"Could you tell me about his beard?"

Owen grabbed his hat off the table. "It was like my hat, but black, I think."

"A knit cap."

"Yeah…it looked kind of silly."

"A beard beanie," Reid said.

"A beard beanie. What's that?" Claire asked.

"It looks like a beanie, but it's for your beard."

"Okay…" Claire pulled out her phone and did a quick

Google search before stumbling on what she was looking for. "Like this?"

She slid the phone in front of Owen.

"Yeah. I told him it was funny. Wearing a hat on your chin. He said it kept his face warm."

"Do you remember what else he said to you?" Stacy asked.

"He said my mom had been in an accident."

"A car accident?"

"I think so. He was going to take me to the hospital to see her."

"Did he tell you what Grandma was doing?"

"He told me his friend was going to pick her up after she paid for the tacos."

"And then you drove to the cabin?"

"He gave me a video game in the car and told me I could play with it if I stayed very quiet."

"So that would have been extra fun for you."

"Yeah. He told me Mommy said it was okay."

"Did you go to any other cabins?"

Owen shook his head. "Nope, just the one where Mommy found me."

Claire made a mental note of the discrepancy. The couple who'd called in saying they'd seen Owen had given the police a different location than where he was found. Was that just a mistake or something significant?

"Did he talk to anyone on the phone while you were in the car or here at the cabin?" Stacy asked.

"I don't think so. He just kept checking his watch."

"Owen, I'm going to show you some photos to see if you can recognize him."

Owen just shrugged. "Okay."

Stacy went through a number of photos Claire had

given her of men who had been at the fires and matched the height and weight description her mother had given the police.

"Do you see him here?"

"No, but it's hard to tell."

"Because of his beard?"

Owen nodded. "They don't have beards."

"That is true. Did he ever take off the cap?"

"Nope. He told me his face got cold in the winter."

"What else did he tell you, Owen?"

"He told me that my mom was better and that she was going to meet us there. And then she did."

"Yes she did. She was very happy to see you."

"But she's not hurt."

"No, your mother is fine. You don't have to worry about her at all."

Owen scrunched his lips together. "I remember something else."

"What's that, Owen?"

Claire sat up in her chair and leaned forward, praying her son had something that would help them find the man who'd taken him.

"He had a tattoo."

"That's great. Can you tell me where it was?"

"I don't really know what it was, but it was here," Owen said, pointing to his wrist.

"So he had a tattoo on his wrist. Was it an animal?"

"No."

"Do you think you could draw it?"

"Maybe."

Claire pulled out a piece of paper and a pen from her bag and slid it in front of Owen.

Owen took the pen, tapped it on the table, then starting drawing something. "It looked like...fire."

Claire glanced at Reid. It made sense. An arsonist with flames on his wrist.

"Does that help?" Owen asked.

"Very much. You did great. Thank you for helping out." Stacy shot him a wide grin. "I'm going to talk to Deputy O'Callaghan about getting you a badge."

"Cool."

Stacy stood up. "Can I borrow your mom for a minute, Owen? We're just going to be in the hall."

Owen reached for his hot chocolate and took another sip. "That's okay."

Reid followed the women into the hall where Detective Kaufman was waiting for them, but this time, Claire stayed close enough so she could still see Owen through the doorway.

"The information he gave will help," Detective Kaufman said. "We'll add the tattoo to the BOLO."

"Good."

"I understand you want to stay here in Timber Falls?" the detective asked.

"At my parents' ranch," Reid said. "Griffin and the captain believe they'll be safest there."

"Are you sure your parents are okay with that? Are *you* okay with that?" Claire asked.

"Of course. I want you both safe."

She studied his face, trying to read his expression, but there was no emotion or warmth behind his words. He was just doing his duty as Owen's father. Just like she'd always feared.

And there wasn't anything she could do to take back the past.

She'd almost lost Owen, and now because of what she'd done, she'd lost Reid for the second time.

Claire opened the car door, then kissed Owen's sleepy face. "Hey, buddy…can you wake up? We're at the ranch I told you about. They've got horses and a pond. You're going to love it."

Owen's eyes widened. "Can I ride a horse?"

"Well, tonight we're going to go get settled into the house and go to bed, but we'll be here for a few days."

"I think we can manage a horse ride tomorrow, if it's okay with your mom," Reid said. "Do you want me to carry him in?"

Owen slipped out of her arms. "I can walk."

Claire marched up the front steps behind Owen, then stopped at the top of the stairs, suddenly feeling as if she were heading to an execution, not just into the father of her son's childhood home. That was a problem. But how was she going to face Reid's family with them knowing she'd never told them about Owen?

She tried to steady her breathing, but the anxiety lingered. Still, Owen was okay and that was all that mattered right now. Reid would come around, and if he didn't…well…they'd go on with their lives and be okay, as they always had.

Then why is your heart begging to let him in?

She glanced at Reid, wishing he'd at least talk to her, but he'd been quiet the entire trip back to the ranch. The problem was, he had every right to ignore her. Maybe things would have been different all those years ago when she'd first found out she was expecting Owen. If she'd simply told Reid the truth then, they'd be in a different place today. But it didn't matter now, because she hadn't done that. And she couldn't force Reid to love her and Owen.

Marci met them at the doorway with a broad smile. "You must be Owen."

Owen nodded. "Yes, ma'am."

"I'm Reid's mom. And if it's all right with your mom, I have some fresh chocolate chip cookies in the kitchen waiting for you."

"Mom, can I?"

"Yes. Just remember your manners."

"I'm going to put you in Reid's old room," Marci said to Claire. "It's a good size, and we set up a cot in there for Owen."

"Thank you." Another pang of guilt raised its ugly head. "I really appreciate it."

"Of course. I've also got tea and coffee."

"Some tea sounds great. And thank you for letting us stay."

"I'm sure Reid has told you that I've always loved a house full of people." Marci turned to Reid. "Why don't you get Owen some cookies and milk, then maybe introduce him to Sasha. And Claire, you go sit down in the recliner. I'll bring you some tea in a minute."

Claire watched as Owen followed Reid into the kitchen, seemingly right at home, then she headed into the living room where Christmas lights were twinkling on the tree. Her son needed a father figure in his life.

He needed Reid.

She sat down in the chair, knowing she should be helping in the kitchen, but exhaustion enveloped her. Today had pushed her to the limits emotionally and left her reeling, but Owen was safe.

Thank You, God.

She couldn't forget she had so much to be thankful for.

"How are you holding up?" Marci asked, setting down a cup of tea beside Claire.

"I don't think I realized how tired I am until I sat down."

"From the little I've heard about your day, you've been through a lot. I'm so sorry."

"I just want to thank you for letting us stay." Claire picked up the tea and took a sip. "You've gone far beyond the call of duty."

"We're happy to have you. Owen's absolutely adorable. You've done a great job raising him, and I know it can't be easy being a single mom."

"My mom helps out a lot. Traveling for my job has made it a bit more challenging, but I enjoy my work and am home most of the time."

"Your mother's coming down too, isn't she?"

Claire glanced at her watch. "She should be here any minute, actually. She wanted to get Owen and me some of our clothes."

"Good." Marci cocked her head. "Can I ask you a personal question?"

"Of course." Claire pulled the warm mug against her, not missing the serious tone in Marci's voice.

"I know I'm prying, but Reid is Owen's father, isn't he?"

"I…" Claire nodded, taken off guard by the question. But at least everything was out in the open. No more secrets. No more hiding. "Yes. He is."

"I can see it in Owen's eyes." Marci walked to a bookshelf next to the fireplace and pulled out an album. "He looks exactly like Reid when he was five."

Marci set the album in front of her.

Claire ran her finger across the photo of Reid sitting up proudly on a horse. "Wow. You're right."

Marci sat back down next to her. "Does Reid know?"

Claire nodded her head. "He found out today, not in a way I ever imagined it happening."

"I'm assuming you had your reasons for not telling him."

"I thought I did." Claire sat silently for a moment, trying to collect her thoughts as the guilt continued to pulse through her. "I found out I was pregnant with Owen about a week after he broke things off between us. I listened to some advice that convinced me I was doing the right thing by keeping it from him, and that Reid would only be saddled with the two of us and in turn become resentful. I didn't want him to get back into a relationship with me out of a sense of duty, but now... now I don't think I did the right thing. I'm so sorry I didn't tell you. Reid missed all these years of being with his son, and you missed out on being grandparents."

"I can't imagine how hard it must have been for you."

"I never stopped thinking about Reid, or questioning what to do, but every time I wanted to tell him, I would stop, and the more time passed, the easier it became to keep that secret. Now I've realized that the secret I was trying to keep doesn't help anyone, it only can hurt." Claire turned back to Marci, worried about her response, but all she saw in the older woman's eyes was compassion. A compassion she didn't deserve. "I really am sorry. I kept your grandson from you. I never should have done that."

"I'm assuming Owen doesn't know?"

"Not yet. But I'm going to tell him."

"I think you should. He deserves to know who his father is. The time is going to come, as well, when he starts asking questions, and avoiding the truth is just going to get harder."

"I know, but Reid's angry at me." She set her tea down beside her, as the anxiety returned. "He doesn't think I did the right thing."

"He's hurt and rightly so, to be honest."

"I know."

"What else is wrong?"

"I'm scared. The arsonist is still out there, which means Owen is still in danger. I just wish we had more answers."

"No matter what my son is feeling right now, I know he's going to do everything in his power to keep you safe. Both of you."

"I know." Claire looked out the window where Owen and Reid were playing with Sasha on the front porch. "I just feel like I've hurt so many people. And I'm worried that he's going to feel obligated to walk back into my life. That's what I've always wanted to avoid."

"And then resent you for it?"

Claire nodded.

"I understand what you're saying, but Reid is just as much involved in this situation as you are. You can't forget that."

"But I don't want him to feel trapped. That will only hurt all of us."

Marci sat back in her chair. "This is butting my head in where it doesn't belong, but I'm just going to say that he's never looked at anyone the way he looks at you."

Claire started to respond, then stopped. Just like Reid, she was going to need time to process everything that had happened and what him knowing about Owen meant for her future. For their future. She'd spent the past six years expecting Reid to reject her if he ever found out. The thought that he might care about her—and Owen—both relieved and terrified her.

"So what am I supposed to do?" Claire asked.

"For now, I'd give him some space. I'm not going to make you any promises, but I know Reid. He's not one to hold a grudge. Give him time to deal with his hurt and what it's going to mean to have you back in his life."

"And if he doesn't want me in his life?"

"Don't go there. Not yet. Just give him some space."

Owen bounced back into the living room in front of Reid, clearly on his second wind. "Can we get a dog, Mom?"

Claire chuckled. "We'll talk about that later, but right now, it's time for you to get washed up and head on to bed."

Owen scrunched his nose. "You mean a bath?"

Claire smiled. "I do indeed."

"Do I have to?"

"Owen…"

"Yes, ma'am."

Marci stood up and set her hands on her hips. "If you want to come with me, young man, I'll get you set up with a towel and a toothbrush."

"I'll be there in just a minute, Owen." Claire waited for the two of them to leave the room, then turned back to Reid.

"I just… I wanted to thank you for letting me stay here. I know this isn't easy."

"It's fine. I'm just glad he seems to be okay."

"Me too, though I've got a friend back in Denver

I want him to see. She helps kids deal with traumatic stress."

"I think that's a good idea."

Claire glanced down at the floor, hating the stark barrier that had come between them. "I'm sorry, Reid. You have to know that. I truly am."

"I really wish you'd stop saying you're sorry. What bothers me the most is that if none of this had happened, I still wouldn't know about my son. You're only telling me how sorry you are because I found out and now it's in the open."

"Reid—"

"Would you have told me?"

"Maybe. Eventually. When Owen started asking questions."

"I wish I could say this is all going to end well between us, but right now, I just can't get past the fact that you never told me the truth. How am I ever supposed to trust you again?" Reid grabbed his coat off the back of the chair where he'd left it. "I need to get some air. You have plenty of people to make sure you're safe."

"I'm not the only one needing protection. He tried to hurt you. Twice. You could have been killed in that wreck," she said trying to keep the desperation out of her voice. "Besides...this is the perfect time to get to know Owen. He'd like that."

Reid turned back to her. "What do you want out of this, Claire? A happy family?"

"Reid..."

"I can't just forget everything that happened. That I have a son. That you never told me."

"Have you forgotten that when you broke up with me,

it was because you weren't ready to commit. You didn't want a family. What was I supposed to do?"

He looked down. "I don't know."

"Surely we can find a way to make this work. Even if it's just for Owen's sake."

"I want Owen in my life, Claire, because he's my son, but I can't do this. I can't do *us*."

She started to say something, then closed her mouth. It didn't matter what she said. He was right. She watched him turn around and leave the house, slamming the door behind him. No matter how hard she tried to make things right with him, this wasn't something she was going to be able to fix.

FIFTEEN

Reid swung the ax down as hard as he could, splitting a log in half. He tossed the wood onto the pile, then grabbed another log. He'd had to get out of the house and away from Claire and her constant apologizing. Maybe she'd had some justification in not telling him, but he still couldn't get past the anger.

How am I supposed to forgive her, God? I'm just not sure I can do it.

He swung the ax again, letting his muscles redirect the anger boiling inside him.

"Whoa…slow down." Caden came around the corner of the barn and held up his hands. "We're going to have enough wood for the next decade the way you're going at it."

"I just needed to blow off some steam."

"Actually, I could hire you. I struggle to find people willing to do the grunt work. The pay's not great, but you get free room and board."

"Very funny." Reid took a step back and tightened the grip on the handle. "I guess you heard the news."

"No. Just that you might need someone to talk to."

"Claire is staying here, with her son."

"And that's a problem because…"

"Because he's my son."

"Okay." Caden glanced to the pile of chopped wood. "This is all suddenly making more sense."

"She lied to me, Caden. I have a son, and she made the decision on her own that I didn't need to know. And now…" He picked up another log and set it down on the block of wood. "Now, I've missed five years with my son. I thought she knew me enough to realize that I would have been there for her. I wouldn't have just walked away."

"Maybe that was why she didn't tell you."

Reid swung the ax up, then split the log down the middle. "What do you mean?"

"If I remember correctly, the two of you had a few issues back then and you broke up with her because you weren't ready for a family. Maybe she felt if she told you she was pregnant, you would have felt trapped."

"She pretty much just told me the same thing, but I would have done the right thing."

"Exactly. You would have married her, because you wanted to do the honorable thing, but she always would have wondered if you stayed around because you loved her, or because you felt like you had to."

"Whose side are you on?"

"I'm not taking sides, just helping you look at the situation."

Reid tried to push back the growing frustration and slammed the blade of the ax into another log. A thin piece of wood flew past him, hitting the barn wall. "That's no excuse for not telling me. I just don't think I can forgive her for this, Caden. The more I think about it, the angrier I get. That's my son in there. She had no right to keep him a secret."

"So what are you going to do about it?"

Reid dropped the ax to his side. "What do you mean?"

"Well, the way I see it, you have several options. One, you could tell her you don't want her or Owen in your life. Two, you could simply fulfill your role as a father, pay child support and take him to ballgames a couple times a year. Or three, you could see if things might actually work out between the two of you this time. You did love her once and maybe you're both in a place now where a relationship might work. The problem is you're both too stubborn to see it."

Reid blew out a sharp breath. "This isn't me being stubborn. And besides, we're not going to take up from where we left off all these years ago. We're both too different."

"Would you consider moving forward if she wanted to? Because it's pretty clear you still feel something for her, and there's a good chance she feels the same way. I've seen the way she looks at you."

Reid shook his head, wishing things felt as cut-and-dried as Caden made it sound. "The problem is that it's not just about Claire and me anymore. We have a child that she kept from me, and I'm not sure I can get past this."

"But if you could?"

"Nothing justifies what she did. And this is always going to be between us." Reid turned to face his brother. "How can I ever trust her again? I don't think I'll ever be able to."

"Forever is a long time, and you don't have to decide today. Why not just give it some time? Get to know Owen. Spend time with him and Claire. Just see where things go."

"I don't know if I want to see where things will go. The person I spend the rest of my life with has to be someone I can completely trust. And Claire...she's not that person anymore."

"Reid—"

"Forget it. I honestly don't want any more advice. Forgiveness is a whole lot easier when you're not the one having to do it."

Caden held up his hands. "All I'm saying is give yourself some time to work through what you're feeling and give her a lot of grace. I don't think she ever meant to hurt you."

"It doesn't really matter what she meant or didn't mean to do. We're in this situation because she didn't have the courage to tell me the truth."

"Hold on. This *situation* isn't all her fault and it definitely isn't Owen's fault."

Owen. His son.

Reid swallowed hard. None of this was Owen's fault. But how was he supposed to build a relationship again with Claire? He couldn't just turn off his feelings at will. Forgiveness, if he ever could get to that point, wasn't going to come easy.

"I think I'm going to get Sasha and go home," Reid said. "Griffin promised to have a patrol car here tonight, and you and Dad will be around. She doesn't need me here. It just makes things awkward for everyone."

"That's where you're wrong. I think you need each other."

"What I need is for none of this to have ever happened."

Caden grabbed a set of keys out of his pocket and tossed them to Reid. "I also think you should stay, but feel free to take the extra truck until you get yours sorted out."

Reid bit down on his lip, regretting his choice of words, but that didn't mean he didn't wish all of this would simply go away. He pulled off his gloves and headed to find Sasha. His feet crunched on the snow. He didn't need Claire. He hadn't seen her for over five years and now he felt like everyone just expected him to let her back into his life—and his heart—like nothing had happened. But that wasn't realistic. She'd made the choice to keep him out of her life, which meant he didn't owe her anything. End of story.

I think you need each other.

Irritation surfaced as his brother's words kept repeating in his head, no matter how hard he tried to shake them. But it was easy for Caden to tell him what he should do. Caden wasn't the one having to deal with the consequences.

But Owen wasn't simply a consequence. He was a sweet little boy who deserved a father and parents who loved each other. But was that something he'd ever be able to give his son?

Reid's phone went off. He pulled out his phone and read the text from Captain Ryder.

Just received a confirmed lead on our suspect. I know it's late, but I need the two of you to meet me back at the B&B.

Claire was standing in the middle of the living room when Reid stepped in. "Reid?"

"I just got a message from Captain Ryder."

"So did I." She hesitated. "I know we need to go, but I'm not sure I want to leave Owen."

"My mom would be happy to watch him, but I understand. I can go. You don't have to."

"I need to, but it's just that I—we—came so close to losing him."

He saw the fear in her eyes and felt his anger lessen a notch. "I really do understand."

Claire's hands fisted at her sides. "I have to come. Finding who's behind this is the only way we are going to put an end to this nightmare. The only way to keep Owen safe."

"Are you sure?"

She nodded. "Let me go tell Owen and your mother what we're doing, and then we can go."

Claire sat in the passenger seat while Reid sped down the highway toward the B&B. He hadn't said anything since they'd left, but as guilty as she felt, nothing she'd said or did had made a dent in the wall Reid had put up between them.

"Is this how it's going to be from now on?" she asked. "You just don't talk to me."

He let out a sharp sigh. "I hope not, but you've had almost six years to figure all this out, and I've had… I don't know…six hours. Maybe I'm going to feel different at some point, but for the moment, it's a lot to process."

"Fair enough." She pressed her lips together, trying not to say anything that would make things worse, but nothing was worse than the deafening silence hanging between them. "Is there anything you'd like to ask me?"

"Besides more clarification on why you didn't tell me?"

"I tried to explain how I felt." She shot up a prayer for wisdom, needing all the help she could get. "Listen, Reid, if time is what you need to process all of this, then I'll give it to you. Whatever you need. I know it's going to take time for both of us to figure out what's next."

"Yeah. It is."

But she had no idea what the next step was going to be, and to be honest, she wasn't even sure what she wanted anymore. Lingering thoughts of the three of them becoming a family were fading quickly. She'd lost that dream a long time ago. Still, she didn't want Reid to shut her out. Somehow they were going to have to find a way forward without hurting her son. Because Owen had to be her priority at the moment.

And if Captain Ryder was correct, all of this would be over soon.

Reid pulled into the driveway that led to the B&B, then slowed down to let a cat cross in front of them. Worry and fear pressed against her chest as the house came into view. She'd come to Timber Falls intent on taking down an arsonist. Instead, over the course of a couple of days, her entire life had been flipped upside down.

The captain's SUV was parked outside the house, where the only light on was in the living room, which wasn't surprising. The B&B was closed and the Grahams were currently staying in town. Reid parked next to the SUV, then headed up the sidewalk to the house beside her. The air was still tinged with the smell of smoke. She was here because they needed answers, but all she wanted to do right now was see what the captain had found and get back home to Owen.

"I see you got the captain's message."

"Shawn?" Claire stepped into the living room that had been mostly spared from the fire. "We did. Where is he?"

"Actually, the captain isn't going to make it. It's just me."

"I don't understand." She glanced at Reid. "Where's the captain? He's the one who told me to come here."

"He'll live, though he might have a headache for a while."

"What did you do to him?"

"Just borrowed his phone." Shawn pulled out a gun and aimed it at them. "Come stand by the staircase, both of you, and don't try anything stupid. I'm a really good shot."

A really good shot?

What was he talking about?

"Shawn, what do you want?" Reid asked.

Claire glanced around the room, trying to figure out what was going on. This couldn't be happening. She'd known Shawn for years, seen him as a friend.

He tossed Claire a long piece of rope. "Tie him to one of the wrought-iron stair railings, and do a good job, because I'll be checking."

"Shawn…" She didn't know what his plan was, but getting loose from the staircase would be almost impossible, and if Shawn was planning to set the house on fire…

"Just do it!"

She moved next to Reid and mouthed, *I'm sorry.*

"We'll get out of this, Claire."

But would they?

"You don't get it, do you?" Shawn said, stepping up behind her.

"Get what? Because no, I don't know what's going on, but you need to put the gun down. That isn't going to help. Just tell me what you want."

"Tie him up tight, or I'll have to shoot the father of your child."

A chill ran through her. This wasn't the Shawn she'd gone to school with, or the one who'd gone out looking for her son. She glanced up at him. Or had he been behind all of this and fooled them the entire time?

"Tell us what you want," Reid said.

"Isn't it clear? Claire's the only thing I ever wanted. Ever since high school."

"Me?" She finished securing Reid, then took a step backward. "I don't understand."

"Of course you don't, because you never noticed me. I was always stopping by your mom's house when we were in high school, but really I just wanted to see you."

"Because we were friends."

Shawn shook his head. "But I didn't want us to just be friends. I wanted more than that."

"All these years…" She faced him, fighting to grasp what he was saying. "Why didn't you just tell me how you felt?"

"Would that have made a difference? You never saw me as anything but the boy next door, so I decided to become a firefighter like you. I thought maybe if I did something good with my life, you'd notice me. But instead you fell for Reid."

"Shawn I—"

"That's why I decided to start the fire at the Reynolds farm."

"*You* started that fire?"

"It was brilliant, wasn't it? A way to get you to come to Timber Falls. All I had to do was leave a couple clues and it worked."

"But I still don't understand. You didn't have to burn down a building to see me. You could have come to Denver."

"I needed to get you down here, then I needed a way to save you. That was my plan, anyway. And with some digging, I was able to figure out how to do that."

The pieces of the puzzle were slowly starting to fall into place. "The locked door at the B&B. That was you?"

Shawn nodded. "I wasn't going to hurt you. I never wanted to hurt you. Just lock you in the room and then save you."

"But you didn't try to save me," she said. "I could have died."

"I tried, but then the owner almost caught me setting up things in the house, and he locked me out. Everything went wrong after that. Thankfully I was able to doctor the security footage, but still…"

He motioned for Claire to stand a couple of feet away from Reid. "You're next."

"What about the drone?" Reid asked. "I'm guessing that was you too."

"It's ironic that the captain actually sent me to Denver to learn about them. There are so many ways fire departments can use drones. Their thermal cameras can find people, they can help with investigations, assess risks with aerial views of the fire…"

And this had all been to get her attention.

Claire resisted the urge to fight as he secured her to another one of the stair railings. She'd been working this case for months, and in coming to Timber Falls, had never thought about a copycat. But Shawn had used his connection with the fire department and found things out like the antique lighters. And she'd played right into his hands.

"When the fire here didn't work," Shawn said, "I had to get Reid out of the way. Because you're always in the way. And no matter what I do, she always goes to you. The handsome fireman and father of her child…"

"And you took Owen?" Clare asked.

"I didn't hurt him. I would never do that. I just wanted us to be a family. If you just would have stopped and looked at me. You would have seen that you could trust me more than him." He waved the gun at Reid.

"And this…this is you trying to prove I can trust you?" Claire asked. She worked to slow her breathing and calm her panic. There had to be a way out of this. She wasn't going to let Owen lose both his mother and his father today. Because Shawn wasn't going to get away with this. "Just tell us what you want."

"One last fire. Your real arsonist will be blamed for this."

"You know who the real arsonist is?" Claire asked.

"It's funny, because a few weeks ago, while research-ing the case, I inadvertently discovered who's behind the fires. He'd disguised himself well—the guy in the hoodie—but I managed to figure it out by tracing his tattoo."

"So he never was here in Timber Falls at all."

Shawn laughed. "All of you saw what you wanted

to see. A doctored photo from the fire put the arsonist here in Timber Falls. Temporary tattoos convinced you *he'd* taken Owen, not me. And now, with the information I left as crumbs for the authorities, they'll find him, and he'll go to prison for those fires and for this one. He was already going to prison for life, so this is just what he deserves. And I might not get the girl, but at least I'll be a hero. The man who brought down the Rocky Mountain Arsonist."

"So if you can't have Claire, no one can?" Reid asked. "Is that what you're saying?"

Shawn turned to Reid. "That wasn't my original plan. The first time I tried to run you off the road I didn't realize she was in the vehicle with you. So I backed off. But yeah, if I can't have her, no one can."

Claire fought the terror as Shawn grabbed two jerricans of fuel and started dousing the room. "Don't do this, Shawn. Please. My son… I don't want him to grow up without parents."

"Why not? I did, and look how I turned out."

"Reid—"

"You don't think Reid really loves you, do you?" Shawn stepped in front of her while she tried to undo the rope on her wrist. "Things wouldn't have worked out with him. He moved on from you a long time ago, and even if some of those feelings are still there, it's not like he can really trust you after you kept a secret like that for all these years. That's not something easy to forgive, is it Reid? She lied to you, didn't tell you that you have a son. That…that is unforgivable."

"Shawn, please…"

Shawn finished pouring the gasoline across the wood

flooring. "I learned you can't force people to love you. No matter how hard you try."

Reid pulled on his wrists. "She made the best decisions she could at the time."

"Are you really going to come to her defense? The woman who never told you about your child? I wouldn't if I were you. Because I've learned the truth about her. She's not a good friend. Not really."

"They're going to figure out you were behind the fires and Owen's kidnapping." Claire struggled for something…anything that might bring Shawn to his senses, but from the empty look in his eyes, it was too late for that. Still… "Shawn listen to me. Please. Murder's a different story. You don't want to do this."

"No, they won't figure it out. They'll believe it was the arsonist, and he really did set all those other fires. No one will ever know what I did. Because no one has any idea of my involvement."

Shawn pulled a lighter out of his pocket.

"Shawn—" The room began to spin around Claire. Surely things weren't really going to end like this.

God…please…

"Stop begging," he said, catching her gaze. "It doesn't look good on you. And besides…it won't be so bad. Most people don't die from the flames, but from the smoke inhalation. It will quickly incapacitate you, then suck up all the available oxygen. You're both firefighters. You know how the particles of smoke can penetrate the respiratory system and then find their way to the lungs. Some are just irritating, but others are toxic. And if the air is hot enough, one breath can kill you."

Why hadn't she ever seen this side of Shawn? He'd always seemed like a good friend. She'd even let him watch Owen at that cabin. Bile from her stomach burned her throat. Her life couldn't end this way. She tried to shift her wrists, but he'd tied them so tight.

He walked up to her and ran his thumb down her cheek. "It's over, Claire. Anything we could have had together…everything I imagined happening between us one day… You had your chance, but it will never happen."

"Don't do this, Shawn. Please."

"Too late."

He used the lighter to start the fire. First the curtains, then the couch were consumed. She could smell the smoke. Things couldn't end this way. She needed to be there for Owen. She couldn't let him grow up without his parents. And as for Reid…

"Goodbye, Claire."

Shawn dropped the lighter onto a chair, then left the house.

SIXTEEN

"Claire…"

She stood near Reid, her hands secured to the wrought-iron railing, while flames continued to move closer. How had they missed that Shawn was the one behind all of this? He couldn't begin to wrap his mind around the man's motivation, but for right now, all that mattered was getting Claire out of here alive.

"Claire, are you okay?"

"Yes, but I can't get my hands undone," she said, not even trying to mask the panic in her voice. And he couldn't blame her. Flames crackled around them, ravenously licking up the accelerant soaking the fabric around the room. It wouldn't be long before the entire structure was on fire and started to collapse. In another couple of minutes, there would be no way out.

"Hang in there," he said. "We're going to get out of this. I'm almost loose."

He was hoping that Shawn's cockiness would be his downfall. In the man's rush to tie them up, he'd forgotten to check the rope around Reid's hands, and Claire had tied it loosely, which gave Reid the advantage. But with his wrist brace, he was struggling to use enough strength to undo the knots.

What if he couldn't manage to get free?

Heat pressed closer against him. He glanced at Claire, while the shifting rope chafed his wrists. He hadn't wanted things to end like this between them. He'd just been so shocked that she'd never told him the truth. So shocked, he couldn't see himself ever trusting her again. But no matter the anger he was still holding onto, he didn't want anything happening to her—or to Owen. No matter how betrayed he felt by what she'd done, a part of him had never stopped loving her. He just wasn't sure it was going to be enough to make things right with her, even if they did somehow manage to survive this.

The smoke thickened around them. He needed something to cover his mouth, but with his hands tied in front of him, it wasn't possible. He tugged harder on the loose piece of rope, praying that if they couldn't get free, someone would at least notice the smoke and come see what was going on. The fumes filling the room were beginning to affect his breathing. As a firefighter, he knew all too well the dangers of fire—how quickly it spread and how unpredictable it could be. He had to get them both out of there in the next minute or neither of them were going to make it.

"How could Shawn have done this?" Claire's raspy voice rose above the crackling flames.

Reid didn't have answers, but his question was how they had both missed this. It wasn't the first time he'd heard of a firefighter arsonist. While the vast majority choose their career for the right reason, to make a difference, there were some who betrayed the trust of every firefighter. From what he knew now, Shawn, it seemed, had been desperate to play the hero in order to get Claire's attention. And somehow they'd missed it.

The rope loosened again. A second later, he was able to pop one hand free. He quickly tugged the bindings off. "I'm free."

His wrists were raw from the rope, and his side ached, but there was no time to deal with the pain.

Claire was coughing as he rushed to help her. "Hurry, Reid. The ceiling is about to collapse."

Wood splintered above them as he fumbled in the semidarkness to free her wrists. No matter how angry he was at her, he would never leave her. He had to get her out and put an end to this nightmare.

"Hurry, Reid." She was choking on the smoke and her tone was frantic.

Don't let me lose her now, God. Not this way.

Things might never work out between the two of them, but Owen needed a mother. And Reid wanted to get to know his son.

Seconds later, she was free.

He managed to find his phone in his jacket pocket. He flipped on the flashlight, then grabbed her hand and pulled her toward the front door. "Cover your mouth as best you can and stay low."

A grating noise of splitting wood cracked above them. Seconds later, a large beam dropped from the ceiling, hitting the floor in front of them and blocking the way. Flames exploded. He pulled her back and held up the light, searching for an alternative way out. There was a narrow path to the left of the fallen beam…

They made it to the door, but when he turned the handle, it was locked. He unlocked it and shoved on the door, but it was jammed from the outside.

They were going to have to find another exit.

"There's a side door." He pulled her with him as he fought to avoid flames that were spreading rapidly to anything the previous fire hadn't destroyed.

We need You to step in, God, and get us out of here.

He stumbled over something, but managed to catch his balance, still holding tightly to her hand, but he wasn't sure he was heading toward the other door. The smoke was too heavy. He flashed his light again. This time he found it. He reached for the handle, then shoved the door open. Moonlight streamed through the smoke surrounding the house that was starting to collapse around them. He needed to get her as far away from here as possible.

They made it to the tree line, several dozen feet away from the burning house, then he bent over next to her, breathing in deep gulps of air. He hit the emergency option on his phone to call 911.

A clicking noise to his left caught his attention. He shifted his torso, then froze. Shawn stood holding up his phone in one hand and a gun in the other. "You just can't admit when you're defeated, can you?"

"Shawn…" Claire took a step forward, but Reid grabbed her hand and pulled her behind him.

Reid slipped his phone into his pocket without hanging up the call, and shouted over the crackling roar of the fire. "It's over, Shawn. Time for you to put an end to this."

"I don't think so. My original plan might not have worked exactly the way I'd hoped, but it's definitely not over. All I have to do is shoot you both, then dump you in the middle of the inferno raging behind me. The Rocky Mountain Arsonist will still be blamed."

"You're wrong," Reid said. All he needed was enough

time to stall until help arrived. His 911 call would immediately activate a search that could trace the GPS on his cell phone. They just needed to stay alive until then. "This won't change anything."

"Why not? You changed everything when you got involved. You couldn't just step aside and let me win her over."

Reid stared at the light on Shawn's phone. While flames devoured the B&B in the background, Shawn was filming them, just like he'd filmed them with the drone and filmed the wreck. Maybe Reid had been wrong. Maybe reasoning with the man was futile. It was as if Shawn had lost touch with reality, and if he couldn't be the hero he wanted to be and win the girl, he was convinced his only option was to have everyone pay.

Reid squeezed Claire's hand, then lowered his voice. "When I tell you to run, I want you to run for the tree line."

"Reid—"

"No arguments, Claire—"

"What are you saying to her?" Shawn stepped forward.

"I'm just making sure she's okay. You say you care about her, but you don't act like it."

"I do care—or at least I did. But I know now she'll never love me. That is why things have to end this way."

"So you want her dead? That doesn't make sense. We're supposed to protect those we love."

"I tried to protect her, tried to show her that I cared, but every time you got in the way."

"I hear what you're saying, Shawn, and I'm so sorry I hurt you," Claire said. "But you need to put down the gun. Please."

Shawn's gaze shifted "Stop trying to distract me."

Part of the roof caved in behind them, sounding like a clap of thunder.

Reid shoved Claire away from him. "Now."

"Claire!"

Shawn shouted her name, then raised his weapon to fire a shot. Reid heard a click from the firing pin. The gun was jammed. Shawn threw down the weapon and ran toward Reid, before tackling him. Reid's body screamed out in pain as his head hit the ground, but he forced himself to roll over and get up. Shawn came at him again, this time throwing a punch, but Reid managed to dodge the impact. He took a step forward, then slammed his fist into Shawn's jaw. Shawn staggered backward, but he wasn't done fighting. Lights flashed as Shawn's second punch hit its mark on the side of Reid's face. Stars erupted, then everything went dark, and he fell to the ground.

Claire let the piece of firewood she was holding drop to the ground as Shawn slumped in front of her. Chest heaving, she kicked his gun out of the way. She wasn't even trying anymore to ward off the panic. Reid had told her to run, but when she'd turn around and seen the blow Shawn had delivered to Reid, she'd instinctively raced back to help. Now Reid wasn't moving. If he was dead… No, she couldn't think that way. He had to be okay.

Smoke filled her lungs as she fumbled to pull out the rope she'd shoved in her pocket as they'd run from the house—the same rope that Shawn had used to tie her up. She thrust her heel against Shawn's back, then pulled his arms behind him before he could move, grateful for her training in the academy. She'd just never imagined the need to restrain a fellow firefighter.

Sirens wailed in the distance as she finished tying the knot securely, then hurried toward Reid. He was lying on his side, groaning, but at least he was conscious.

She crouched down next to him. "Reid… Reid, please tell me you're okay."

He rolled onto his back, then looked up at her. "I think he just knocked the wind out of me, though my head is killing me. Where is he?"

"I saw you go down and had to come back. It might not have been the most conventional method, but I hit him over the head with a log, then tied him up."

"Looks like I owe you my life, then."

The sound of sirens intensified as a firetruck pulled up to the house followed by two county sheriff's vehicles. A second later, Captain Ryder jumped out of the passenger seat of one of the cars, followed by Griffin.

"Captain Ryder?" Claire hollered at the man, while the firefighters moved into position to put out the fire. She was sure it was too late to save the house this time around.

"Reid… Claire…are you both okay?" Griffin asked.

"I think so," Claire said, then turned to the captain. "What about you, sir?"

"Besides just having been knocked out I'll live, but I want to know what's going on."

"Long story short," she said, "we just caught a copycat arsonist."

"A copycat arsonist?"

"Shawn." Reid pulled the man up onto his feet. "He set the fires here and at the Reynolds farm. And tonight, he tried to kill both of us by tying us up in the house and setting it on fire."

"I don't understand," Griffin said.

"We'll explain everything, but for the meantime, he needs to be taken in," Reid said.

Claire walked up to Shawn as one of the deputies properly cuffed him. "I might not have looked at you the way you wanted me to, but I still thought you were a friend."

Shawn just turned his head and ignored her. Claire frowned. At least he couldn't hurt them anymore.

"Get him out of here," Griffin said. "We're going to need statements, but I want you both checked out by a doctor first."

"Can we at least stop by Shawn's apartment on the way?" she asked. "Shawn told us he figured out who the real arsonist was, and that he planned to use this fire to get rid of us and to frame him."

"That was his plan?" the captain asked.

Claire nodded. "Exactly."

"We'll take care of searching his place—"

"But—"

"No buts," the captain said. "The two of you are going to the hospital."

Claire started to argue, then stopped, knowing that between the three of them she'd never win. An hour later, she stepped into the lobby of the ER where Reid and Griffin were waiting for her. Hopefully Griffin had some news, but she realized all she really wanted now was to get back to her boy and get a good night's sleep.

"It looks like the doctor gave you both a clean bill of health," Griffin said as she walked up to them.

"What about your head?"

"I've got a bad goose egg, but no concussion."

"Good. What about Shawn's apartment?" she asked.

"They're not finished, but you were right," Griffin said. "We have enough evidence to put Shawn away for a very long time."

"What did you find?" she asked.

"There was the knitted beanie beard and the cap and glasses Owen told us about, along with packaging for the temporary flame tattoos he wore when he grabbed Owen."

"No wonder Owen didn't recognize Shawn," Claire said.

Griffin hesitated, glancing at Reid. "It looks like he not only altered the security footage, but also doctored some of the photos from the B&B fire by photoshopping in the real arsonist as further 'proof.'"

"And?" she pressed.

"There were also dozens of photos of you hanging on the wall," Griffin said. "Apparently he really was obsessed with you. On the bright side, though, local PD in Littleton just picked up our real Rocky Mountain Arsonist. His name is Stephen Montgomery."

Claire glanced at Reid. "So all of this really is over?"

"We're going to have to sort through all the evidence we have and separate the real from the fake, but from what I've seen so far, I think we have enough to close the case."

"Plus you and Owen are safe," Reid said. "That's what really matters."

Claire bit the edge of her lip, wishing he'd tell her what he was really thinking. There was a part of all of this that was far from over. She knew he still hadn't had time to process the situation completely, or to forgive her for keeping him in the dark all these years, but all she could do was accept responsibility for her actions. He might never want to see her and Owen again. Those were the consequences she was going to have to deal with.

God, You know I've tried to rededicate my life to You, but waiting for Reid to forgive me...if he even does... isn't going to be easy. I honestly just don't know what else I can do.

Griffin's phone rang and he excused himself and stepped away.

"I just spoke to my dad," Reid said. "Your mother's at the ranch, and Owen's fine."

"I'd like to go back to the ranch tonight since it's late, but I think we'll plan to head home to Denver tomorrow."

"I figured that was what you were going to want to do. Griffin's offered to drive you to the ranch now."

"Okay." Clearly, Reid didn't want to be around her if at all possible. "Look, I know it's going to take time for you to process all of this, and I want you to know I'll give you all the time you need. But if you'd like to see Owen at some point..."

"I would. But I'm also going to need some time to figure all this out."

"That's fine. He doesn't know who you are, so maybe it's good to keep it that way for now."

"Okay."

She started to say she was sorry again, but stopped. Nothing she could do would fix the past or repair things between them. The only thing she knew to do now was walk away, without looking back.

SEVENTEEN

Claire set a cup of coffee in front of her mom, then sat across from her at the kitchen table with her own mug. Owen was playing in the living room with Legos, close enough that she could see him, but far enough away that she and her mom could talk in private. Intense feelings of overprotectiveness were a consequence of everything that had happened. She hoped that would fade as time passed.

"You've been quiet since you got back from Timber Falls," her mother said, taking a sip. "I'm glad you were given some time off, but I've been worried about you."

"I've just been thinking about a lot of things." Claire spooned some sugar from the glass bowl and added it to her coffee. Coming back to Denver hadn't been easy, but she knew it was time she told her mom the truth. "I made the wrong decision when I found out I was pregnant. I should have told Reid the truth from the beginning. Trying to cover up what happened has only made things worse. He deserved to know he had a son."

"I agree."

Claire set the spoon down. Her mom's response was not what she'd expected. "You do?"

Her mom added some more cream to her own coffee and nodded. "I spent some time talking to Reid's mom while I was at the ranch, and I realized that I'm the one who was wrong."

Claire sat back in her chair. "This isn't what I was expecting you to say."

"I know. But I've had a lot of time to think over the past few days, and convincing you not to tell Reid... well...for that I'll always be sorry."

"Thank you. I appreciate your saying that. I just wish it wasn't too late. Reid doesn't want anything to do with me."

Fear had kept her from doing the right thing all those years ago. Fear of the future. Fear of rejection. And she couldn't lay all the blame on her mother. She'd been the one who'd made the choice to not tell Reid.

Her mom's gaze dropped. "That might be true now, but Reid isn't like your father. I was so convinced you'd end up in some horrible custody battle over Owen if you told him, that I let my fears supersede my common sense. I never should have pushed you into keeping Owen from Reid. But that said, I honestly believe that given time, he'll come around."

"But what's that going to look like?" Claire asked.

"I don't know, but what I do know is that you both care about Owen and putting his well-being first no matter what happens between the two of you. Reid just needs time to figure things out. You dumped a lot on him."

Claire tried to hold back the tears that had threatened to erupt ever since she'd returned home. "I know it's going to take time. He wants to be a part of Owen's life. I'm just not sure he wants to be a part of mine."

"Which is why I'm sorry. I really am. I never should have projected my situation onto yours."

"In the end, though, it was my decision, and I've decided no matter what happens, we'll be okay. I wouldn't have made it to where I am without your help, and we'll get through this, as well. My faith is strong, and while Reid might not have forgiven me for my choices, I know God has. And that has to be enough for the moment."

She glanced at Owen, who was still playing on the other side of the living room, and wished it was as easy to truly believe the words as it was to say them.

"I'm proud of you," her mom said. "I hope you know that. And if Reid decides not to be a part of your life, he has no idea what he's missing out on."

Claire laughed. "Spoken like a true mom."

"Listen, I promised to take Owen to the park before the temperatures drop again. Do you want to come along? I know you haven't wanted to let him out of your sight these past few days."

Claire started to say yes, then hesitated. At some point, she was going to have to let go. "I think I'll stay here. I have some things I need to do around the house. Just make sure he's bundled up."

"He'll be fine. I promise."

"I know."

Claire was regretting her decision thirty minutes later when the doorbell rang. She rushed to the front door, her heart automatically braced for bad news. Instead, Gwen and Tory stood on her front porch holding a decorated sack from a bakery down the street.

"Gwen… Tory…hi."

"I hope you don't mind us stopping by unannounced,"

Tory said. "We drove up to the city for some last-minute wedding stuff and wanted to bring you something."

"Of course not. Come in," Claire said, then shut the door behind them to keep out the cold. "Would you like some tea or coffee?"

"Yes, but we really can't stay. We need to get back to Timber Falls before dark." Gwen handed Claire the small sack she was holding. "We wanted to check on you and bring you some macaroons. They'll be at the wedding."

"Wow…thank you. Owen will love these. Well…" She laughed, still not sure what to make of the visit. "So will I."

"Gabby would have come, as well, but Mia came down with a cold and Gabby wants to make sure she's better by the wedding."

"How many days now?" Claire asked.

A blush crossed Tory's face. "Three. I'm so ready."

"And everything is coming together?"

"It is." Tory glanced at Gwen before turning back to Claire. "There is another reason we wanted to stop by. I wanted to invite you and Owen to the wedding."

"Wow…that's so sweet of you, but—"

"I know you're worried about things being awkward with Reid," Tory rushed on, "but I'd really love to have you there."

"I don't know—"

"We'll be honest with you," Tory said. "We're also doing this for Reid."

"Reid?" Claire's stomach dipped. "Why? I don't think he has any desire to see me again."

"That's where you're wrong. That man has moped around ever since you left."

"I'm sure that has nothing to do with me."

"I don't know exactly what happened between the two of you," Gwen said, "but I know he's never gotten over you."

"She's right," Tory said. "We saw the way the two of you looked at each other. You made mistakes, we get it. We all have. But don't let that scare you away from what could happen."

Except the chance of anything happening between them had long since passed. And seeing him again was only going to make things worse. If they could get worse.

"You care for him, don't you?"

"Of course, but…" Claire hesitated again, then decided to be totally honest. "The truth is, I can't stop thinking about him. I dream about him at night, see him everywhere I go. But that…it doesn't matter. I have to respect his wishes, and he made it pretty clear he doesn't want anything to do with me."

"He was hurt," Tory said. "You know that. But I think he just needed some time to process the situation. And I think seeing you again would change everything."

"I appreciate the two of you stopping by to talk to me, I really do, but I need to go on with my life. Without Reid."

"Just promise us you'll at least consider coming."

Claire frowned, determined not to grasp onto something that would never happen. "Just because you've both found your happily ever after romance, doesn't mean everyone will."

"Happily ever after doesn't mean it's not a hard road to get there," Gwen said. "And the two of you have a difficult past to overcome. I get that. But I'd really hate for you not to work things out just because one—or both of you—are too stubborn to see that you really love each other."

"But I broke his trust. There's no undoing the past."

"Trust me. He might have gotten hurt in all of this, but he never stopped loving you," Gwen said. "We all make decisions in our life where sometimes the consequences are tough. You've had to raise Owen as a single mom and I can't imagine how difficult that has been. And we're not saying everything will be perfect from here on out."

"But what we are saying," Tory said, "is that if you do have feelings for him, don't run away from them again. Marci and Jacob love you, and we'd selfishly like to see you as a part of our family."

"You might be getting a little ahead of yourselves. Like I said, I'm not sure he likes me, let alone loves me at this point."

"Well, it's up to you, but the invitation stands."

"Thank you."

A minute later, Claire shut the door behind the women, blocking out the gust of wind seeping into the house. She was glad Owen wasn't here for the moment. Every time she saw his face, she saw Reid. The problem was that no matter how much she fought it, a part of her wanted to be in Reid's life, wanted to be a part of his family. But was that even possible?

The door to the garage banged open. "Mom!"

"Hey, sweetie." Claire shoved aside her emotions and smiled as Owen flew around the corner. "Did the two of you have fun?"

"We did."

"I'm glad."

Owen threw his arms around her. "I like having you home from work."

"And I like being home." She knelt down in front of him, hoping she wasn't going to regret what she was about to say. "Owen, do you remember when we went to that wedding a couple months ago?"

"And I got to wear a suit?"

Claire nodded. "How would you like to go to another wedding?"

"Where is it?"

"In Timber Falls, at the O'Callaghan ranch."

The familiar feelings of fear pressed toward the surface, forcing her to question the decision. But if she couldn't go for herself, she would go for Owen.

Reid moved the stepladder over another two feet, then climbed up to change a lightbulb hanging in the front of the chapel that was already decorated for today's event. Afternoon sun filtered through the stained glass windows onto sixty-year-old wooden pews that had been draped with evergreen boughs and red ribbon.

His grandfather had built the small chapel with its stone flooring and wooden crossbeams as a quiet refuge, a testament to both his craftsmanship and his faith.

"It looks great in here," Griffin said as he walked down the center aisle of the chapel, already dressed in his tux. "But what does Tory have you doing now? The wedding's in just over an hour."

"I told her to put me to work this week, and she's done just that. This time it's two burned-out light bulbs."

"Looks like putting you to work turned out to be a good idea, but you've definitely been distracted these past few days."

Reid finished replacing the light, then started back down the ladder. "I guess I'm not used to taking this much time off, though I had no idea planning a wedding could be so time consuming."

Griffin laughed, but quickly sobered. "Something tells me that your restlessness has nothing to do with the wedding and everything to do with Claire."

Reid set the burned-out bulb on the front pew, then dusted off his hands.

"Don't even try to deny it," Griffin said.

Reid blew out a sharp breath. "Fine. I can't get her out of my head, no matter how hard I try. And Owen... he's my son, but in every scenario I come up with, it just...it feels so complicated."

"What's complicated?"

Reid shrugged, not sure how to put his feelings into words. "What if she ends up marrying someone else one day? Where does that leave me?"

"Do you love her?"

"I know I loved her once, but now...we're very different people."

"What does your gut say?" Griffin asked.

It was the question he'd been trying to ignore. Walking away was the easy way out. It meant he didn't have to deal with his feelings or the consequences of what might happen. But as much as he fought it, his heart refused to deny he had feelings for her.

Reid leaned against the ladder, then rested his hands on his thighs. "When we were in that fire, trying to make our way through the smoke and chaos, all I could think about was getting her out. And how if anything happened to her... I just knew I didn't want to live without her."

"Then why don't you tell her that?"

Reid hesitated at the question. "Because all of those feelings don't really matter if I can't trust her. What she did was inexcusable. She didn't tell me about our son, and had no intention to. If Shawn hadn't said something to me, I might never have known."

"You don't think she would have told you eventually?"

"Does it matter? Owen is turning five this month, so no, I don't think she had any intention of telling me."

"Finding out you have a son is a lot to take in. I'll admit that."

"But you still think I'm making a mistake."

"I think you both made some wrong decisions years ago, but making another bad decision isn't going to fix things. The way I see it is that you've been given a second chance."

"A second chance for what?"

"She didn't tell you about Owen, but don't forget you'd just broken up with her. Think about the situation from her side. She didn't want you to feel trapped or forced to get back together for the wrong reasons. She's probably just as scared as you are."

Reid shook his head. "But we're talking about a child. Our son. Maybe she was worried I would get back together with her for the wrong reasons, but on the other hand, he's my son and there's no way to get around the fact that I deserved to know about him."

"Maybe you'll never have a romantic relationship again, but don't you want to be a part of your son's life?"

"You know I do."

Reid started up the aisle of the chapel, but Griffin stepped in front of him. "Love is always a risk, but trust me…taking that leap of faith is worth it. Now that I'm getting married to a woman who completes me, I can't imagine it any other way."

Reid let out a sharp sigh. He'd spend a lot of time growing his faith, which was why he wasn't the same person he had been all those years ago. And he knew Claire had changed, as well. But did that mean they were meant to be a family?

He leaned against the end of the old pew. "I'll admit I miss her. Maybe I'm even still in love with her. But I'm struggling with getting past the whole trust part."

Griffin waited for him to continue.

"Owen deserves a mother and a father, and I want to be a part of his life, but that doesn't mean I'm not struggling to trust her again."

"All I know is what I've seen between the two of you. When you look at her, you're totally lost."

Reid heard what his brother was saying, but he didn't want a relationship with Claire simply to right a wrong. He pulled out his phone and stared at the photo she'd sent him of their son.

But if that was what he really wanted, why was his heart screaming at him to run after her?

Fifty minutes later, Reid tugged on the black bow tie, then turned around and saw Claire walk into the small vestibule with Owen. Reid sucked in a breath and pressed his hand against his chest. She'd worn her hair down so it lay softly against her shoulders and was wearing an emerald-green dress that swirled around her ankles.

She shot him a shy smile and waved.

"Claire…" He stepped around a couple who had just

walked in, but all he saw was her. "I didn't know you were coming."

"I'm sorry. I… I thought Tory told you."

"No, but…wow…you look beautiful. And you, young man," he said, turning to Owen, "are quite handsome in that suit."

"Thank you." Owen scrunched up his nose. "Why are you wearing a flower? I thought flowers were for girls."

"It's called a boutonniere for men and a corsage for women. People wear them on special days like weddings."

Reid bent down, pulled off his boutonniere and pinned the rose on Owen. "How about that?"

Owen glanced up at Claire. "Does my mom get a flower?"

"I think I can find one for her."

"It's fine." Claire shook her head. "Tory and Gwen stopped by my house and invited me, but now I'm not sure—"

"Oh, Claire… I'm so glad you and Owen came." Gwen rushed up to them in her red bridesmaid dress and pulled Claire into a hug before stepping back. "We have a bit of an emergency."

Claire glanced at Reid. "What's wrong?"

"The ringbearer came down with the chicken pox this morning. We decided not to worry about it, but now that Owen's here…" Gwen pressed her lips together. "Would you mind if Owen takes his place?"

"No. As long as he doesn't mind."

Gwen turned to Owen. "Would you like to be a ringbearer in the wedding?"

"What does that mean?"

"You just walk down the aisle holding a pillow and a ring, and keep it very safe. And when it's over you can eat cake."

Owen shrugged. "Sure. I can do that."

Gwen kissed him on the top of his head. "You're a lifesaver."

Owen started to follow Gwen, then stepped back in front of Reid. "Are you going to be my daddy?"

Reid tried to push down the lump of emotion. "Would you like me to?"

Owen cocked his head. "Yeah. I think you'd make a good dad."

He smiled, then ran to follow Gwen, leaving Reid alone with Claire.

"I… I'm not sure how to respond to that," he said.

"You never know what an almost five-year-old is going to say," she said, clearly feeling as awkward as he was.

Violin music started playing in the background. Reid glanced toward the doors leading from the small lobby into the chapel.

What does your gut say?

Griffin's question replayed in his mind, and suddenly everything seemed clear. He might still have all of the same doubts and fears, but maybe that was okay. Because the truth was that Claire wasn't the only one who'd made mistakes in their relationship. She'd made it clear that she wanted something permanent with him and he'd been the one who'd run. He'd told her he wasn't ready for marriage and a family. Could he really have expected her to have done anything else?

"We need to talk," he said.

"The wedding's about to start."

"We've got five minutes until I have to be at the front with Griffin." Reid took her hand and pulled her outside and onto the side of the chapel while guests continued to trickle in. "I've been trying all week to convince myself that I don't need you in my life, that you would be better off without me, but I can't get you off my mind."

"I—"

"Don't say anything. Not until I'm done. Please." If he didn't say what he was feeling now, he might never be able to.

"Okay."

"First, I think Owen's right about my making a good dad, and second, I owe you an apology. Your mother called me and told me, like you did, about how she convinced you not to tell me about Owen. So here's the thing. If I've learned anything over the past few years, it's that God is the God of second chances. I know He's done that in my own life, and I think you've seen the same thing. You were put in a difficult situation when you found out about Owen, and while I wish you would have come to me, I can understand why you did what you did."

Claire's eye's widened. "You can?"

A light snow started falling, dusting her hair with snowflakes. He reached up and brushed one off her cheek. "I'm not saying it doesn't still hurt, but yeah, I think I can."

"But you told me you couldn't ever see yourself having a family."

"Do you know why I said that?"

She shook her head.

"I said that because I could never see myself with anyone but you." He cupped her face in his hands. "And that hasn't changed. I don't want to live my life without you and Owen."

"But I don't want you to be in our lives just because you feel guilty or obligated."

He brushed his lips across hers, lingering for a few seconds while he pulled her against him. "Do you believe me now?"

A soft smile settled across her lips. "That's a good start."

"There are going to be obstacles, I know, and we're going to have to tell Owen the truth, but I lost you once and, in the process, lost our son. I don't want to lose you again."

"I don't think I ever stopped loving you either. If we could be a family…"

Reid let out a low whistle. "As unexpected as all this is, I think I'm finally ready to have a family if it includes the two of you."

"Well, it's about time the two of you figured out you were still in love with each other," Caden said, walking up to them, before shooting Reid an apologetic look. "Sorry to interrupt, but we do have a wedding about to start."

"I just need another minute," Reid said.

"Thirty seconds," Caden said before heading back inside.

"You need to go," Claire said, resting her hands against his chest. "We'll have plenty of time to talk after the wedding."

Reid grasped her hands and laced his fingers with hers. "I know, but now that we're being honest with each other, I'd really like to kiss you again."

The smile that crossed her lips was the only answer he needed.

He leaned down and kissed her, this time knowing he'd found what he'd been looking for—the missing pieces of his heart, wrapped up in the presence of the woman he loved, their son and the promise of a future filled with forgiveness, redemption and hope.

* * * * *

If you enjoyed this thrilling story from Lisa Harris, don't miss the other O'Callaghan brothers' stories:

Sheltered by the Soldier
Christmas Witness Pursuit
Hostage Rescue

Available now from Love Inspired Suspense.

Find more great reads at
www.LoveInspired.com.

Dear Reader,

I can't believe that Reid and Claire have brought the O'Callaghan brothers' stories to a close. I also can't begin to tell you how much I've enjoyed writing their stories and exploring the commitments of family, honor and loyalty, and delving into the themes of sacrifice and going beyond the call of duty.

We all know that life is full of twists and turns. Sometimes, like in a suspense novel, it takes you places you'd rather not go, but it can also bring joy you didn't know was even possible!

Today, I'm praying that wherever you are in life at this moment, you will feel God's presence and peace in your life.

Because of Him,
Lisa Harris

Get 4 FREE REWARDS!

We'll send you 2 FREE Books plus 2 FREE Mystery Gifts.

Love Inspired Suspense books showcase how courage and optimism unite in stories of faith and love in the face of danger.

FREE Value Over **$20**